COPYRIGHT

STRIPPED

A FERRO FAMILY NOVEL

By

H.M. Ward

www.SexyAwesomeBooks.com

Laree Bailey Press

STRIPPED

A FERRO FAMILY NOVEL

CHAPTER 1

CASSIE

Bruce claps his big beefy hands at us like we're misbehaving dogs. "Come on ladies! Hustle! The bachelor party isn't going to be much fun if we never get there. Damn, Gretchen, you aren't even dressed, yet?"

She laughs like he's funny, even though Bruce is as far from funny as a person could get. He's the bouncer at the club and on nights like tonight, he comes with us to keep the guys from getting handsy. Some rich brat out on Long Island rented us for the night. There are seven of us going to perform on stage, plus the stripping wait staff, and dear, sweet, Bruce.

Gretchen is piling her long golden hair onto the top of her head and securing it with a long bobby pin. She's strutting around half naked, as if we like looking at her. She smiles sweetly at Bruce and waves a hand, bending it at the wrist like he's silly. "Please, I'll be ready before Cassie even finishes lacing up her corset."

She tilts her head in my direction as I fumble with my corset hooks. Every time I manage to hook one, another comes undone. Whoever invented the corset should be burned at the stake. The stupid thing might look cool once it's on, but getting into it is a whole other matter. Add in the fact that mine is a real corset—meaning it has steel boning—and breathing isn't something I can do either. I got this thing because it was authentic. I thought that meant it had period fabric or grommets or something cool. It turns out that authentic means metal rods built into the bodice, guaranteed to bruise my ribs. Fuck, I hate this thing, but I refuse to throw it away—it cost me three weeks' pay at my old job. Plus, it's not like I wear it every night. We only pull out the good stuff on holidays and for special events like this.

Bruce turns his head my way and looks like he wants to pull out his hair. I'm nearly dressed, except for this contraption. My ensemble includes the candy apple colored corset, lace-topped thigh highs, and a delicate little G-string, coupled with heels that could be used as weapons. If I ever get mugged wearing these shoes, you can bet your ass that I won't run, not that I could. These are the things I think about when I make my purchases. Can this purse do some damage? Maybe I should skip the leather Dooney and grab me that metal no-name bag with the sharp corners. My roommate and I live across the street from a drug den. Don't even get me started on that. I know we need to move, but knowing it and affording it are two different things. In the meantime, I buy accessories that can be used as weapons.

Glaring at her, I reply, "Gee, thanks, Gretch." My fingers push the next bit of metal through the grommet. This one stays put.

She bats her glittering lashes at me. "No problem." Gretchen is tall and lanky with a larger-than-life super model thing going on. I hate her. She's a bitch with a capital B. It's all good, though. She hates me, too. It's difficult to be hostile toward someone that likes you. Gretchen makes it easy to hate her guts.

Me, I'm not a supermodel. I'm nothing to look at—my mom drilled that into my head a million times. I'm completely average with sub-par confidence, but I can act. I can fake it so that once I hit that stage, I'm as good as the rest of the strippers.

No, I didn't dream of being a pole dancer when I was a little kid, but my life took some wicked turns and here I am, dealing with it. There are worse things I suppose, although I won't be able to think of a single one when I'm letting a bunch of pervs rake their lusty eyes over my naked body. The truth is, I hate this. I'd rather be anywhere else, doing anything else. The gynecologist's office, sign me up. Root canal, no problem. I'll be there early and with a smile on my face. Anything is better than this.

Bruce lingers in the dressing room for too long, staring at his watch. His thick arms are folded over his broad chest as he watches the second hand tick off the passing time. He ignores Gretch's gibe at me. I may be newer, but I pull in a lot more cash and that's what the boss likes—lots of money. As long as I keep doing it, I have a job.

I finally get my corset hooked up when Beth walks by. She's already wearing some frilly satin thing. "Hey, Cassie. Do you want me to lace you up?"

Tucking a piece of hair behind my ear, I nod. "Yeah, thanks." She laces me in, pulling each X tightly, cinching me up until I can barely breathe. "Tight enough?"

I try to inhale deeply, and can't because the metal bars inside the fabric won't permit it. I nod and press my hands to the bodice, feeling the supple satin under my hands. "Yeah, tighter than that and I'll pass out—or pop a boob."

She laughs, "You're the only one who worries about stuff like that. You're so cute." She ties off the strings and tucks them in before swatting my back when she's finished. My boobs are hiked up so high that I can't see my toes when I look down. I grab my robe and wrap it around me as we head to the cars. It's going to be a long night.

————

The ride to the party is short. We're on the north shore of Long Island, not too far from the coast. There are tons of old homes with huge lawns and even bigger estate houses nestled out of sight between towering oaks and pines. The place hosting the party looks like a castle. We pass through the gates and drive around to the side of the house. The van stops and we're told the usual—go wait in the servants' wing until it's time.

Beth and I walk inside, shoulder to shoulder, whispering about the garish wealth that's practically dripping from the walls as we walk inside. Gretchen and a few other girls trail behind us, chattering about what kind of tips they'll make tonight. A party like this can line a girl's pockets for a month if it goes well, but for me it'll do more than that. You see, I'm the main event, the mystery girl in the pink room— the bachelor's private-party dancer. While my coworkers are off in the main hall, I'll be earning the big bucks. That's the main reason why Gretchen hates my guts. Before

I came along, she was the top stripper around here.

It's getting late, which means the party is well under way. Beth picks up a tiny sandwich off a tray as she walks to the back of the bustling room. "You think this guy knows what's coming?"

I shrug. "Like it matters, anyway? When's the last time we were sent away?"

"Uh, never." She pops the food in her mouth and chews it up.

I'm leaning against a counter top with my elbows behind me, supporting my weight. "My point exactly. Guys are dicks. They commit to marrying a woman, but this kind of crap the night before the wedding is okay." I roll my eyes as I make a disgusted sound, and straighten up. All of a sudden I'm talking with my hands and they're flying all over the place, "Tell me, why would a guy want a lap dance if he's in love? You'd think he'd only want his bride, but that never happens. He's always happy to have an ass in his face."

"Well, your ass is pretty awesome, or so I've heard." Beth smirks at me and glances around the kitchen. We're in the way, but there isn't anywhere else for us to go yet.

"Guys suck, that's all I'm saying."

"I know. You've said it a million times." She makes a *roaring* sound and shakes her fist in the air before turning to me and grunting, "Men. Evil."

"You're an idiot." I smile at her, trying not to laugh.

She points at me and clicks her tongue. "Right back at you, Cassie."

Bruce waves us over to the other side of the kitchen. "Cassie, Beth—follow me." We duck out behind him and follow the guy down the hall and slip into a little room. It's been done up in pale pinks with silver curtains, similar to the room I work in at the club. Since this is a party, Bruce added another dancer and I got to choose. While I work the stage at the front of the room, Beth will work the floor.

Bruce points a beefy finger at the stage and says to us, "Take your places, and remember that this client is the shit. Pull out all the stops, say 'no' to nothing. You got it?"

We nod in unison. The stage is elevated off the floor, with a few steps up at either end. It looks like the stage is new, built just for me. People usually rent those gray, make-shift stages that wobble when walked on, but not this guy. They spared no expense. The walls are lined with pale pink silks and illuminated from the floor. Clear tables flicker around the room with pink flames dancing within. It's seductive. The colors blend together, reminding me of pale flesh and kissable pink lips. As I climb the steps up the side of the stage and head to the silvery tinsel curtain, I call back to Beth. "Who is this party for again? And why is he the shit? I must have missed the memo."

She laughs as she's examining one of the lights within the glass table. It looks like fire, but it can't be since it's pink. She looks up at me. "Dr. Peter Granz, and he's the shit because he's a Ferro. Hence the swank party." Beth looks up when I don't answer.

I rush at Beth, nearly knocking her over. My jaw is hanging open as worry darts across my face faster than I can contain it. "Ferro?"

"Yeah, why?"

I'm in melt down mode. "I can't be here." I glance around the room and look at the door longingly. Before I make up my mind to run, I hear male voices approaching. Fuck! My heart pounds faster in my chest. If he's here, if Jonathan sees me—the thought cuts off before it finishes.

I'm ready to bounce out the window when Beth grabs my wrist and hauls me to the front of the room. She shoves me behind the curtain and hisses in my ear, "If you freak out now, Gretchen will steal your job. Snap out of it. Whoever this guy is, he isn't worth it."

The tinsel curtain in front of me flutters, but it conceals both of us for the moment. The male voices grow louder until the door is yanked open. The curtain rustles and I'm in full freak-out mode. He can't be here. He can't see me like this. At the same time, Beth's right. I can't skip out. Bruce will run me over with the van and there's no way in hell they'll ever give me another cent.

I stand there, frozen, unable to think. Every muscle in my body is strained, ready to run, but I don't move. My bare feet remain glued to the floor as I smash my lips together.

Then, I hear it—that voice. It floats through the air like a familiar old song. Oh God, someone shoot me. I can't do this. "You don't know what you're talking about. What guy wouldn't want a party like this?" Jonathan is talking to someone in that light, charming, tone of his.

"Uh, your brother, Peter. Do you know the guy at all? He's going to act like he loves it and get the hell out before you can blink." Glancing through the curtains, I can see the second man. He has dark hair and bright blue eyes like Jonathan. The only difference is their posture. Jonathan has all his weight thrown onto one hip with his arms folded across his chest. The other guy's spine is ramrod straight, like he's never slouched in his life.

Peering at Jonathan through the tinsel, I see a perfect smile lace his lips. "Sean, I know him better than that. Pete is going to love this. It's exactly the kind of party I'd want if I was getting hitched."

"Yes, I know." Sean's voice is flat. He glances around the room with disgust, and slips his hands into his pockets. "Don't say I didn't warn you."

"Oh come on! It's Peter. What's he going to do?"

Sean laughs, like he knows something that Jonathan doesn't. "Don't let that English teacher façade fool you, Jonny. He's as hot headed as I am. No one fucks with him. He's going to consider this a slap in the face, an insult to Sidney. Cancel the strippers before he gets here." Sean leaves the room without another word.

Jonathan Ferro lets out a rush of air and runs his fingers through his thick, dark, hair. The aggravated sound that comes out of his mouth kills me. I've heard it before, I know him too well to not be affected by it. That's the sound he makes when he knows he's screwed up, when he sees that he isn't the man he wants to be. There's always been this wall between Jonathan and his family. I guess he still hasn't gotten past it. Jon paces in a circle a few times and then darts out of the room.

"Holy shit." Beth looks at me and hisses, "What happened between you and him?"

It feels like icy fingers have wrapped around my heart and squeezed. I stare after him and utter, "Nothing, absolutely nothing."

CHAPTER 2

JONATHAN

Why does everyone think they know my brothers better than I do? I'm taking advice from Sean. How the hell did that happen? I'm walking swiftly down the long hallway, chin tucked, not watching where I'm going. The golden wallpaper appears to be glowing in the dim light. I run my hands through my hair and down my neck, and smack into someone.

When I look up, I'm ready to snap. "What the— Oh, it's you."

My closest friend, Trystan Scott, is standing in front of me. The guy is the brother I never had. He's not blood, but he might as well be called a Ferro because he's that loyal.

Trystan's wearing ripped jeans, a button down shirt with the top three buttons undone, and has way too much shit in his hair. "What the hell's going on? I thought the waitresses were supposed to be strippers. That was the coolest idea you've ever had. Imagine my disappointment when I rush out of rehearsal—away from the sexiest woman you've ever seen—and get here to find a bunch of chicks still wearing clothes." Trystan smirks and shoves his hands in his pockets.

I don't bother to answer him before resuming full speed down the hall. I have to find the guy from the club and cancel my awesome plan. Damn it, why does Peter have to be so difficult. Who doesn't want strippers at a bachelor party?

Trystan follows behind. "So, how's it going?" His voice has that teasing tone, which means he knows how well it's going.

"Nice hair," I throw back, and glance at him out of the corner of my eyes. Trystan makes a face and tries to smooth it down, but it doesn't move. "What'd they use, glue?"

His dark hair is sticking up all over the place. It looks like a porcupine toupee. "Something like that. I look like a fucking idiot."

"Yeah, but it's not the hair that does it—it's the make-up."

"Awh, fuck." Trystan swipes his hand across his eyes, trying to rub it off. "I forgot. I had somewhere to be—somewhere with strippers—so I ran over here as fast as I could." He smacks my arm with the back of his hand. "So, come on Jon, what's going on?"

"Apparently this isn't Pete's MO. I'm canceling the girls before Peter gets here. Sean said he'd bolt, that titties aren't his thing."

"Titties are his thing, but he prefers a certain pair." Trystan grins and looks over at me, pressing his hand to his chest. "The ways of the heart are—"

"And what would you know about that? You're a goddamn legend. You've nailed every chick from coast to coast."

Trystan's smile brightens, but it's like there's something he's not telling me. Ever since I met him a few years ago, he's been like that. He doesn't talk about his past much, but I don't blame him. From the papers, I know Trystan's dad beat the shit out of him when he was a kid, but that's about it. The guy keeps to himself, but somehow manages to get pussy whenever he wants. A shy rock star is a fucking oxymoron, but the women fall at his feet. What do I know? Maybe I've been doing everything wrong this whole time. I shake the thoughts away and enter the main room.

The music pounds through the air, vibrating through me. The dim lights make it difficult to see the guy I'm looking for. He should be back in the kitchen right about now. I lean into Trystan. "I'll catch you later."

"Whatever you need, man." Trystan grabs my arm and squeezes. He's saying he's got my back, even if no one else does. The guy might be a train wreck, but he's good people under all that shit.

I slap his back, "Thanks. Catch you in a few. We can hit the bar after Pete gets here, because I'm not walking around sober if there's only guys here." Trystan laughs and agrees to get smashed with me later. You got to love the guy.

I weave through the crowd. There are already some strippers posing as wait staff. A woman with a tray and way too much make-up on her face brushes my side and turns toward me. "Champagne?" Her cleavage is up to her neck and the thin white shirt she's wearing does nothing to hide the black bra underneath. Fuck, she's hot. I almost stop and flirt with her—almost—but I keep walking, because I'm not a total dick. This was supposed to be for Pete. I need to fix this before he gets here.

Sean falls in step beside me. "Tell me that I didn't see Scott at the bar?" Sean hates anyone who wasn't born with the name Ferro.

"Fuck off, Sean. He's my friend."

"He's using you." Sean's jaw is locked tight as he scans the crowd. "You're too naïve."

"You're an asshole." I'm not defending my friendship with Trystan or with anyone else. Sean acts like he knows everything, and he might be right most of the time, but he's wrong about Trystan. "The guy has his own millions. He doesn't need mine."

"He's unstable."

"You're unstable." I flick my eyes over to him.

Sean smirks. "Possibly."

"I can't chat about your mental health right now. I need to find the guy before all these girls rip their clothes off. Where's Pete?"

Sean laughs and points across the room. "He just got here."

"Fuck." I take off through the crowd, cutting through the guys, shoving some aside.

When I push through the kitchen doors, I see him. "Bruce! My man—change of plans."

Bruce is a huge guy and doesn't look pleased to see me. There are half dressed girls everywhere, slipping into their tear off waitressing outfits. Damn, this would have been so cool. Bruce has his thigh-thick arms folded over his chest. He glares at me. "No refunds."

"I'm not asking for one." I stand in front of the guy and feel like a toothpick, even though I'm not. Reaching into my pocket, I feel around for a hundred dollar bill. "I need them to keep their clothes *on*."

He gives me a weird look. "They're not supposed to be waitresses, Mr. Ferro.

They're strippers and are expecting the tips that accompany the occupation."

Okay, I grab a fist full of bills and slip them into his hand. Bruce takes it and sees how much I've given him. I ask, "Maybe they could be waitresses for a couple of hours and then head out?"

"Maybe, but this isn't going to help the girls you hired for the private room. They're expecting tips, and if you cancel them out, they'll have left the club for nothing. You have to make good over there." The guy's voice is dangerously deep.

"Done. I'll go take care of it." I reach out and shake his hand.

As I turn to leave he clears his throat. "And if you'd like this kept quiet…"

I reach into my pocket and slap more cash into his fist. Bastard. The large man grins. "My lips are sealed, Mr. Ferro. A suggestion?" he asks, and I nod as my gaze cuts across the room to the clock. "Keep at least one girl in that private room for your guests. This is a party that people will talk about. You don't want them to think you're a pussy. You've got a reputation that people know about. They expect a little something extra at one of your parties."

"And you know this because…?"

"Because I've got ears, Mr. Ferro. Every man here is wondering what your big surprise will be this evening. You need to keep something for them, don't you?"

I don't answer him, because I know he's right. "Fine, I'll go speak to them. You keep the girls out here clothed."

Bruce laughs and leans back in his chair. "Done."

When I get back to the private room, I push through the doors without really paying attention until I hear a voice—that voice. It's like being hit in the face with a wall of cold water. Whatever thought I had in my head is gone. Wide eyed, I look up and scan the room. Two women are tangled together on the floor, fighting. Well, no they're not fighting, not really. I'm not sure what they're doing, and they have no idea I'm watching.

My heart pounds harder as her voice fills my head and I try to see her face. My body responds the way it used to—that hollow spot in the center of my chest aches, along with my cock. I stare in disbelief, watching two strippers wrestling on the floor, and stand in shock because one of them is Cassie Hale.

CHAPTER 3

~THREE YEARS PRIOR~

JONATHAN

My phone buzzes next to my head. I roll over and look at the screen. What the fuck? Blinking hard, I rub the sleep from my eyes. It's Robyn, one of the only people I know down here. My mother exiled me for thinking with my dick. Whatever.

What are u doing?

Sleeping. I type back and put the phone down. It buzzes again.

Annoyed, I pick it up and read her message. *Lame. Get over here. I have someone for you to meet.*

Yeah, right. Like I'm rolling out of bed and going to the mall. It's too goddamn early. I put the phone down and roll over to go back to sleep, but it buzzes again.

Get up loser!

Fuck off, Rob. A bit harsh, yeah, but it effectively communicated that I'm not moving from this bed.

Okay, I'll hand off the hot girl to some other guy who thinks with his dick.

Not funny. I shouldn't have told her why I was sent down here. My family thinks they can hide me in the backwoods of Mississippi until the whole thing blows over, like what I did was hideous—which it wasn't. I'm not a total asshole.

Wasn't trying to be. At least come say hi.

Not interested. The phone finally quiets and I roll over, intending to go back to sleep when it buzzes again.

I mutter to no one, "Fuck, Robyn. I don't want to meet your hideous cousin—" My words stop as I stare at the picture on my phone. It's some girl I've never seen before. She's got long, soft brown hair, pale skin—like the tone of breasts that have never seen sunlight—with a dusting of freckles across the bridge of her nose, and pink lips pulled into a sexy, sweet smile. Just looking at her makes me hard. I groan and rub my face with the heel of my hands. She's hot and I haven't fucked anyone since

I left New York a week ago, which is way too long. Robyn's working all summer, so my normal fuck buddy isn't around. Blinking the sleep out of my eyes, I look at the screen wondering about the chick in the picture.

Another message comes through. *Totally hot, right?*

Maybe. She's looking for a hook up?

Totally. Be here in 10 or I'm setting her up with someone else.

Fine.

I pull on some clothes and run a comb through my hair, but it doesn't want to lay right. So I rub some gel through it and leave it messy. Whatever. She's lucky to have me. I'm a Ferro. No one tells me no anyway, not for anything. I expect to get there and have this chick falling all over me.

There's only one issue to work out—I need a car. I haven't discussed it with Uncle Luke yet. I'm staying at his house for the rest of the summer. Mom said if I didn't keep a low profile that she'd personally castrate me. Nice, right?

I pause at the top of a long winding staircase. The room below has floor to ceiling windows that look out onto the Ross Barnett Reservoir. The water sparkles in the morning sun, blinding me. Uncle Luke sees me standing around as he eats his breakfast in the dining room below.

"Come on and get some breakfast." He's a tall thin guy with a head of thick, dark hair. He combs it like an eight-year-old, parted on one side, and plastered to his scalp. The guy is wearing a plaid shirt, a pair of khakis, and boat shoes, which means he's planning on spending the day on his yacht. It's one of the many gifts the family has sent him to keep him happy and quiet down here. The Ferro name carries a lot of weight and anyone that messes with it gets shipped off to no man's land.

"Uh, actually, I'd like to head to the mall and buy some clothes. Mom tossed my ass on the plane before I could pack." As soon as she heard about what I did, I was dragged to McArthur Airport and shipped out of state. Now, I'm Uncle Luke's problem. I walk down the staircase and over to the table.

I'm wearing the same outfit from yesterday, which isn't exactly new. It was in the dresser drawer from the last time I was here, and no longer fits quite right. The jeans are way too tight and if they hug my balls any harder my voice will go up an octave.

Uncle Luke takes forever to answer. When he does, he leans back and flashes his perfect smile at me. His mouth is filled with veneers, another present from Mom. "Fine. Take the black car. Keys are in the garage. Jonny, do something stupid and I'll take it out of your ass." Uncle Luke isn't kidding. Mom threatened him, too. If I mess up down here, I don't even want to know what she'll do next. I've never pissed her off that much, but it can be done, and there are secrets that I'm sure she doesn't know. If she did, I'd be disowned and lose my entire inheritance. The Ferro family is wealthy beyond comprehension. When I was a kid, I thought we were rich, but it's more than that. There's power in our name, backed by more money than I could ever spend. I'm not getting disowned. Fuck that.

He adds quickly, before I can walk away, "How are you paying for it?"

I shrug. "Charge card, I guess. Mom locked me out of my accounts."

Luke glares at me like I'm a moron. "Never use credit cards. They'll know your business." I blink at him like he's hit his head one too many times. Luke sighs, explaining, "The government looks at shit like this Jonny, and it's none of their goddamn business. Use cash. Always have cash on you and pay in cash. Period." He reaches into his pocket and takes out his money clip, pulling a few bills and handing them to me. "I'll get your mother to reinstate your allowance. In the meantime, that should be enough for a few things."

I nod and thank him, heading to the garage before he can change his mind or make me wear a tinfoil helmet so no one can read my thoughts. Uncle Luke is a little bit of a conspiracy theorist. It was fun when I was a kid, but now it's just uncomfortable. The guy can ramble on for hours about how the government, aliens, and other assorted groups are out to get us. I get why he was banished—Luke makes the Ferro family look fucking crazy.

But the man does have good taste. As I enter the garage I see three cars—a cherry red Ferrari, a dark blue Sunbeam, and a black Maserati convertible. Score. Knowing Uncle Luke, I figured he'd hand me an old Civic or something, but this is way cooler. I get in the Maserati, put the top down, and feel the engine begin to purr as I start the car. It's fucking orgasmic, the way the machine comes to life.

With a slick grin on my face, I pull out and head toward the mall. The ride is over way too fast. I pull the car into a parking spot and head inside. I don't know where to find Robyn, but it doesn't really matter. The mall isn't that big. I pass a few stores and slip my hands into my pockets.

That's when I see Robyn. She's standing in the center of the corridor, with her full profile visible. She looks good. I haven't seen her in a few years, and I take a few seconds to appreciate the way her body's filled out. She was the first girl I made out with who had real curves. The memory is imprinted on my mind. Soft, milky flesh that was smooth and perfect. Maybe I should just wait for her to get off work and we can pick up where we left off a few years back.

Robyn doesn't see me approaching. Her face has a shocked look on it, with eyes too wide. She blinks over and over, like she can't believe what she's hearing, which forces my gaze onto the chick standing across from Rob, with her back to me. Long dark hair falls down her back in a cascade of spirals, hanging just above a tight ass that's the perfect size. She's not a twig with nothing to grab, which is good. When I'm with a woman, I want to grip her ass and drive into her hard—grabbing a bunch of bones isn't the same thing. A bony ass is an automatic turn off.

Her legs are shorter than I'd like, but they're curvy and connect with a killer set of hips. God, and she has that pale skin everywhere. It reminds me of forbidden flesh—of the places that my tongue will slip over and between later if things go well. She's my type, Robyn was right, and from the back, she's pretty hot.

I step toward them, preparing to pry the new girl off of me, because that's what always happens. Once they find out who I am, they get clingy. That's my only concern at this point. The girl looks like the perfect way to spend my summer, and I wouldn't mind being between her legs for most of it, but I don't know. I'll have to see what level of crazy she's running on before I do anything. I can't make any waves down here. The press can't know I'm here, so this might be a bad plan—but there's no way I'm jerking off for the rest of the summer.

As I step closer, I hear her voice. It's nice, not too high. I hate that squawky, whiny tone. I've nailed some women who talk like that, but I can't stand to listen to them. It's like nails on a chalkboard. Instant revulsion. So, everything checks out. She's hot, has the voice, has the hair, the ass, the legs, the flawless skin, so when I hear her say she's a virgin, I freeze in place.

CHAPTER 4

CASSIE

My jackass cousin is speed-walking in front of me. She hurries through the glass mall doors and talks to me over her shoulder. "It won't be that bad. My shift is only a few hours. You can shop the whole time and then we can meet up and hang out."

I struggle to keep up with her long legs. Robyn is the only person who's even close to my age that I know in this entire state. My mom sent me to Mississippi for the summer to give me a break from the city. Like I needed a break from New York? Please. She was just sick of looking at me. "What the hell am I supposed to do for that long? I don't have money to shop for hours every day. You said you didn't have to work, Robyn."

"Yeah, well, I didn't, but things changed, Yankee. Suck it up." I roll my eyes and mutter things. Robyn suddenly stops short and glances over her shoulder at me. "Don't be mad, but I think I have the solution to your problem." I raise an eyebrow at her. This can't be good. Robyn's solutions typically make more problems. "You have nothing to do, and he has nothing to do…"

"What are you talking about?"

"He's cute, and a friend with benefits is a promise if you hang out with him." I must appear horrified because she gives me a funny look. I'm a couple of years younger than her, barely eighteen. "You've had sex before, right?"

I blink at her like she has two heads. I hiss in a low voice, "No, I haven't and I don't want to. Robyn, did you seriously tell some random guy to come to the mall so I'd have sex with him? Are you insane?"

A slow smile creeps across her face. "Oh my God! You're a virgin! You've got to be kidding me?" She's looking at me like I'm a toddler in a tutu—it's that sweet endearing face. The problem is that she's way too loud. People around us are looking as they pass by.

Just as she says it, a guy with dark hair and blazing blue eyes stops next to me. He's smiling at her as he folds his arms over his chest. "So, I'm here. What'd you want?" The guy is beautiful, like completely and totally stunning. His face is perfection, his arms and chest are sculpted, and those eyes—are they even real? He glances at me like I'm not worth looking at and then back at Robyn. "Who's this?" He jabs his thumb my direction.

"That's my cousin Cassie, the virgin." Robyn is still smiling at me. "Cassie, this is Jonathan Ferro."

Hot guy turns abruptly and cocks his head to the side. His eyes travel over my body inch by inch before returning to my face. "Why is she a virgin?" His face scrunches when he says the last word, like it's horrible that I'm not a slut. "She looks perfectly doable to me."

My jaw drops open. "Excuse me?"

"Well, you do. You're a beautiful woman." His eyes sweep over me again as if he's assessing whether or not he'd have sex with me, which makes my cheeks burn.

He takes in my reaction and smirks. "She blushes. I love that. It's so virginal."

Robyn laughs and looks utterly amused. "I know, right?"

Up until that moment, I was very proud of my virgin status. I wasn't putting out for everyone and anyone, but this guy is rattling me and I only met him a second ago. He's arrogant and cocky and everything I can't stand wrapped up into one beautiful body. "Hello, I'm right here."

"I know," he says. "With that body, I can't see why you'd have a problem, unless…" There's a questioning tone to his voice.

"Unless what?" I'm actually stupid enough to ask him.

"Unless you're into girls." He rubs his jaw lightly and looks me over again with a smile. "Is that the reason?"

"No," I squeal a little too loudly as my face flames redder. People walking by stare at us, which makes it worse. My mouth opens and closes a few times before sputtering, "I haven't done it yet because I wanted to wait."

"Why?" He blinks at me like I'm absurd.

"Until I find the right person."

"You're waiting on purpose?" He glances at Robyn, truly entertained. "Where'd you find this chick?"

Robyn laughs and shakes her head. "She's from your neck of the woods, Jonathan. Don't blame me. I don't think like that."

He grins at her. "I know."

Robyn smiles, and it's obvious they've seen each other naked, then says, "I better get going. You two hang out and try not to kill each other."

"That's why you called me down here? To hang out with the virgin?" He looks horrified.

I hate him. It's hate at first sight. I sneer at him. "I have a name, you know."

He looks at me with a this-can't-be-happening expression on his face. "I'm a self-professing male slut, which means I don't care." Jonathan glances back at Robyn. "What the hell am I supposed to do with her all day?"

Robyn laughs. "Not my problem. Catch you after work, Cass."

I make a mental note to kill my cousin later.

CHAPTER 5

CASSIE

We both stand there staring after Robyn. Jonathan sighs and flicks his gaze my way. I feel it slip over my curves, but I don't look at him. I've never had a guy so openly ogle me like this. It makes my insides squirm. I have every intention of ditching him. I mean, what's the point in trying to hang out with a guy who acts like this?

"My eyes are up here," I say dryly, and fold my arms over my chest. I do it to hide my boobs from him, but he just grins as my arms force the mound of cleavage higher. Damn V neck shirt. I drop my arms and wave a hand at him, "Well, it's been unreal. Catch you later."

Jonathan gives me a twisted smile— one that's equal parts pleasure and surprise. He presses his fingers to his chest and follows me as I turn away from him. "Are you ditching me? After I went to all the effort to come down here and hang out with you. I'm hurt, Cassie, I really am."

I laugh once, and glance over my shoulder at him. He can't be serious? Why is he following me? I notice Jonathan's eyes and the downward glance that I assumed was on the floor—it's not as low as I thought. He's staring at my ass. I stop short and he rams into me. Damn, he's a wall of muscle and toned flesh. When our bodies collide I feel a slight tingling under my skin, like I licked an outlet. I suck in a jagged breath, trying to slow the frantic pace of my heart. Oh, what the hell? My body reacts to this guy like he's my goddamn soulmate, but he's not. There's no way he is. I want more than the stuff he's made of, without a doubt.

Jonathan's hands come up and steady me, holding lightly onto my forearms. Those blue eyes cut right through me and I forget how to think. "Easy there, Cassie." He offers a crooked grin. The vibrato in his voice is gone and he looks as shaken as I feel.

My mind has pulled out the warning siren and is screaming at me to step away from the hot man. I'm rendered mute and unable to move. Our eyes lock and linger way too long. Jonathan's lips are parted, like he wants to say something, but he doesn't. Or can't. I wonder if his heart is racing like mine? It can't be, not if he's screwed every girl in his path, which is the distinct impression he's given.

Jonathan's hands slip off my skin and I remember how to breathe. Sucking in air, I take a step away from him. What the hell was that? Averting my eyes, I speak before I should. My voice quivers slightly and lacks confidence. "I need to go shopping. You don't have to babysit me. I'll find my way around—"

For a moment his features are softened and completely serious. His fingers wiggle at his sides as his hands start to lift. I think he might touch me again, but he slides his hands into his pockets instead. "I don't plan on babysitting you. I'll help you with your shopping and then make you fall madly in love with me…" he glances at his watch and tips his head to the side like he's considering something, "By dinner time. That sounds about right. You'll be a molten ball of lust, unable to tell me no by then." When he glances up, he gives me a boyish smile. It's so smug, so utterly confident, and so completely fake.

I fold my arms across my chest and throw out my hip. "I don't think so."

Jonathan's eyes dip to my cleavage. "I know so. One day with me is all it takes, baby."

Huffing, I turn on my heel and head down the mall corridor, looking for some place that he won't follow. Tampax really needs to add a tampon store in here because right then, I don't see any place that will deter him to that extreme. "One minute's enough for me, thanks."

"Ouch!" He's behind me and catches up, falling in step beside me. "Are you always this feisty?"

"Bitchy, the word you're looking for is bitchy." I don't look at him.

He laughs. "You are not a bitch, not by a long shot. For one, real bitches don't make it sound cute."

Go away, go away, go away! "I'm not cute. I'm—"

He steps in front of me and cuts me off. "You're not cute at all." I stop abruptly and stare at him with my mouth hanging open. He laughs lightly. It's the perfect sound; completely amused, kind, and warm. If a laugh could double as a tender embrace, that's what Jonathan's would do. His voice deepens and sounds completely different when he speaks this time, "You're beautiful, devastatingly so."

I can't tell if he's teasing me or if he's serious. The way he says it, the way his eyes meet mine make me think he's telling the truth, but there's a slight curve at the corners of his lips that makes me think he's playing with me. Those words catch me off guard and seep inside. I hate it. This is no one. He's just some random guy that my cousin called up to have sex with me. He's not serious. From the look of him, he's never serious. I swallow hard and look away.

A light laugh escapes before I can swallow it down, but I don't care. I'm never going to see him again and there's no doubt in my mind that he's just trying to get into my pants. When I look up, my gaze meets his and I step toward him, placing my hands on his chest. My voice is deeper, quieter. My lips form the words slowly, hugging each one tightly. His eyes dip to my mouth as I speak. "So are you. You're exactly my type…too bad you're not a virgin. We could have had something." I wink at him and turn away with a smirk on my face.

Jonathan seems stunned, but he snaps out of it fast enough to grab my wrist. He pulls me back and doesn't let go, which sends a surge of sparks shooting up my arm. A devilish smile is on his face. "Are you seriously tossing me back because I'm not a loser?"

"Virgin and loser aren't synonymous." SAT word. See, I'm smart. I can handle this guy. He probably doesn't even know what it means.

He catches my superior tone and throws back, "Well, that's where you're wrong, because they usually are. It's not everyday that a guy meets a hot girl and finds out that she hasn't had sex yet, because she chooses not to. It's usually because the opportunity was never given to this girl, and as soon as an opportunity prePixsents itself, she'll say yes. So, Cassie Whatever-your-last-name-is, do you want me to show you a few things and punch that V card for you?" He's so smug, so overly confident, that I want to punch him and knock the sly look right off his face, but I'm too busy tripping over my jaw. It's hanging open and I have trouble snapping it shut.

Stepping toward him, I lean in like I'm going to kiss him, but I pinch his cheek instead. "Awh, you're so cute! You think you'd be doing me a favor?" I drop my hand, along with the plastic smile, and roll my eyes. "How very noble of you."

"I know. I'm a noble fellow." He tries to take my hand, but I move. He ends up with my wrist and I feel that tug inside my body again.

The physical reaction to his touch is horrifying because it shoots through me like a bolt of electricity, frying my brain and landing directly between my legs. "You're anything but noble, and no, I'm not interested. I was serious about what I said before."

Jonathan drops my wrist as a baffled expression crosses his face. "You can't be..." I roll my eyes and start walking again. I spot a pink store that repels most guys, so I make a beeline for the front. Jonathan trails behind me. "You're the first chick who's shot me down."

"Good, then maybe you'll learn something."

Jonathan stops walking for a second and then races after me. "I'm sorry, I didn't realize you were trying to teach me a lesson." The infuriating smirk on his lips is still there, bright and beautiful. "You see, I was distracted by your perfectly sinful body. My brain actually exploded back there when you said you only use it for good, which isn't good at all, since that makes you off limits."

I'm smiling, and trying to suppress the grin, but I can't help it. I reach into my purse and pull out a Kleenex. I hold it over my shoulder for him. "Here's a tissue, go clean it up." Every time I try to stop, he laces together some sort of flattery with self-deprecation. Apparently, I'm a sucker for that combination.

He snatches it from me, grabs my shoulder, and spins me around. There's a huge smile on his face as his eyes dart between my lips and my eyes. "Let me convince you. You're so wrong about sex that it isn't even funny. It's not something to be saved in a glass jar. It's hot and sweaty with two slick bodies giving in to one another. It's ecstasy and agony mingling together to form the perfect high. It's not the kind of thing you save. It's the kind of thing you learn to master, and you can't do that with just one guy. Give me the day to convince you that you've got it wrong."

His words rattle me as much as his touch. There's something about the way he says it that makes my stomach twist. I glance away from him with a plastic grin on my face. "And how do you plan on doing that? I'm assuming it's a hands on learning experience? Get over yourself, Jonathan. Not every girl wants you."

He feigns being hurt, but recovers quickly, moving his face way too close to mine, whispering, "I think you do want me, Cassie."

"You're so arrogant."

"You're so uptight."

I glare at him, surprised he said it. "What a dickish thing to say."

His voice is smooth and the words sound intoxicating even though he's insulting me. "What a prude thing to say."

"I'm not a prude."

He laughs softly as his eyes lock on my lower lip. "Ah, that must be the problem, because you're the definition of prude. When Webster was talking to Merriam about that entry, your name came up."

My jaw drops open and hangs there for a moment before a sharp smile cuts across my lips. I'm in his face, so close to him that I can feel his warm breath. "At least my picture isn't in the Wiki entry for male slut."

Jonathan grins and his dark brows lift, like he didn't think I had it in me to spar with him. "Did you even know that term before you met me?"

I fold my arms over my chest, throw my hip out, and cock my head. "I've met a million guys like you. There's nothing special about you. You're a mask of perfection with no substance underneath. You're like every other guy out there who's wanted to get into my panties, and you'll end up like the rest of them as well—rejected. Access denied." As I speak, I drop my arms and step toward him. We're nose to nose, eyes locked, and breathing way too hard. I wonder if I've gone too far. At one point something changed and it felt wrong, but I couldn't shut up. I had to have the last word.

Jonathan blinks those dark lashes slowly, and when he lifts his gaze to meet mine, he notices that I've been staring at his lips. They look so soft, and the way the corners of his mouth curl up into that cocky smirk makes me crazy. The mall noise fades away and I'm only aware of him and me. His voice is barely a whisper. "Kiss me, Cassie."

My stomach flips as every muscle in my body tightens. The pull is there, the attraction doesn't stop just because I don't want it. If anything, his words were like throwing water on a grease fire—everything combusts. I'm too close to him and getting way too hot. Watching him through lowered lashes, I finally turn away.

His hand reaches out and touches my cheek lightly, directing my face back toward him. Jonathan leans in closer, slowly, which makes my pulse pound wildly in my ears. A shiver takes hold of me and rushes through my body. Jonathan's light pink lips are perfect. I'm gazing at them, watching him come closer and closer. When his head tips to the side and I feel his breath on my mouth, panic takes over. A lifetime of choices are about to be wiped away because I want to kiss a stranger in the mall. I turn away just as his lips touch me. Instead of kissing me on the lips, his mouth lands on my cheek.

I'm shaking and can't hide it. This guy is making me come apart at the seams. I'm going to lose my mind if I don't put some distance between us. But God, his lips— when they brush against my cheek, my eyes close and I hold my breath. His touch is so soft and his lips are warm and perfect. He pulls away slowly and looks at me from under dark lashes with those sapphire eyes.

My heart is pounding and I can't think. It wasn't supposed to be like this. He's a goddamn stranger, but it feels like there's a cord between us, pulling us together. Fate couldn't be so cruel. This guy can't possibly be my soul mate, but what I feel deep within protests. It's like I've recognized my other half and he isn't who I thought he'd be. Everything about him is wrong.

I apologize, I'm not sure why. "I'm sorry. I have to go. See you around." I take off as fast as I can without actually running, and this time Jonathan Ferro doesn't follow.

CHAPTER 6

JONATHAN

That perfect ass is swaying hypnotically as Cassie races away from me. I can't think of the last time I had a girl say no. Okay, I can't think of any time a woman has said no to me.

I didn't even get a kiss.

Damn, that ass. I imagine holding Cassie tight, her naked thighs splayed over my hips while squeezing those perfect curves as I rock into her. I can picture her face, the way her head tips back when she moans my name. The daydream is short lived. I'm standing in front of Banana Republic with a hard on. I duck inside and try to force it down, but the dick wants what it wants. Plus the image in my mind was so perfectly sinful that I don't want to let it pass just yet.

The mall sucks. Concentrating, I move between the racks, thinking of why I got sent down here in the first place. My mother's death stare is vivid in my mind, along with her shrill voice. It's enough to make my nuts crawl back up into my body. It works better than dumping a bucket of ice down my pants. Damn, the woman is vile.

I flip through shirts and grab a few. I was literally sent down here with only the shirt on my back. Since I'm eighteen and the family heir, I have money, but not now. Mom froze my accounts, for the time being at least. Apparently, my little stunt was over the top. Whatever. It was worth it. I grin thinking about the pay off and Brittany's perfect little breasts bouncing up and down as she fucked me right before I left. That seems like months ago.

My mind shifts back to Cassie. A virgin. Fuck, that chick is crazy—and hot. How has she not slept with someone? Looking for Mr. Perfect is stupid. She'll never find him. Even if she does, she won't know if they're good together until she does it with him. Some guys can't satisfy a woman with what they were given. The dick, and what he does with it, makes a difference. Sex isn't just about getting off—it's two-sided, which Cassie has no clue about. What a waste of ass.

I think about her all the way back to Uncle Luke's. By the time I walk into my room and toss my stuff on the bed, I know what I want to do. But it'll have to wait. I'm being beckoned. He probably wants to make sure I didn't use any plastic.

"Jonathan, come down here please." Uncle Luke calls up the stairs.

I toss my stuff on the bed and go back down. He's in the massive kitchen, sitting on the counter top. "Hey, Uncle Luke. I thought you were going out all day."

"So did I, but plans changed." His brow is furrowed like he's trying to find the square root of 3. He runs his hand through his hair and seems distressed. "I have to head to Meridian for a few days to take care of something. It can't wait."

"That's fine." Why is he telling me this? The guy usually just takes off and forgets to feed me. If I was a hamster, I would have died last time I was here. Water? Food? Jon who? The man has the attention span of a kid on Pixie Stix. Seriously.

"And you're coming with me."

I laugh, and then realize that he's not joking. "Uncle Luke—"

"Your mother will kill me if I leave you alone here. You'll do something stupid and she'll blame me. I like my gifts, Jonathan. And I get a huge present if I manage to keep you out of trouble." He doesn't look at me.

Fuck. I don't want to go camp out in some trashy motel with Uncle Luke for a week. "I'm not going to get in trouble." Uncle Luke gives me a look that says otherwise. I do the craziest thing I can imagine and tell him the truth. "Listen, I'm not. Remember, Robyn? She's around and she set me up with her celibate friend. I'm hanging out with a girl that doesn't put out. See? I can't get in trouble. There's no one to knock up, and I'll stay away from the press."

He watches me for a second, his dark eyes looking me over like he's wondering if I'm lying. "Your friend won't have sex with you? Is that what you just said?" It takes me a second to realize that he's laughing at me.

I let out an annoyed sigh and press my fingers to the bridge of my nose. "Yeah, so there's nothing I can do that'll piss off Mom."

He's smiling at me. I can feel his amusement from across the room. Luke thinks it's funny. Then he's serious again, pointing his finger at me. "Fine, but if you do something, so help me God—"

"I won't." I lift my hands in a classic stick 'em up pose, palms facing Luke, surrendering. "Besides, my funds have been locked up, so I can't spend more than a couple hundred bucks a day. That's not enough to do anything fun, or press worthy."

He considers me for a moment, while his long bony fingers rub his chin. Finally, he says, "Fine. I'm headed out in a few minutes. Your stepmom, or whatever the hell she is, was looking for you, too. She said she'll call later."

"Laurie?"

"No, the other one—Chantel."

I try to hide it, but the sound of her name does something to me. I nod and turn on my heel. Before I get two steps between us, Luke warns, "If your mother ever finds out about them…"

I glance back over my shoulder. The lie slips through my teeth like liquid, perfectly smooth. "There's nothing to find out. They're just checking up on me." I've gotten so good at misleading people, at making them look the other way. Luke putting the pieces together is something, but fuck that. I can make him doubt it, and then I'll have to make sure they don't call me down here. What the hell was she thinking?

His gaze narrows and rests on mine. "Just because you're the heir doesn't mean you can do anything you like. Anyone can say yes, Jonny, but it's a strong man who learns to say no. Your friend with the chastity belt will do you some good. Keep it in your pants. And if your father's leeches show up while I'm around, they'll get an ass full of buckshot. Got it?" There are enough firearms in his basement to form a small militia. I'm pretty sure he shot at the mailman once because he thought he was under attack. Mom nearly killed him for that one. Since then the postal workers around here don't bring packages to his door.

"Yes, sir." There's nothing else to say. I'm screwed. He knows, which means other people have to know, too. I wonder if I should go on lying to him, but what's the point. Besides, I need someone to talk to. My life has turned into such a goddamn mess. There are layers of lies tangled together so tightly that I have no idea how to yank myself free. It's daunting.

Rubbing my hand over the back of my neck, I look up at him. "It didn't start the way you think it did. I didn't go after them. They came to me. I wouldn't steal my Dad's girlfriend."

"Learn to say no. In the end, it doesn't matter what happened or who started what. It's whether or not you acted in a way that makes you proud. Can you honestly tell me that you can look at yourself in the mirror every morning and be okay with what you did?" Uncle Luke watches me, but my gaze doesn't lift from the floor.

There's no excuse for what I've done and I've felt guilty about it since it first happened. I did say no. I did send her away, but she didn't listen. Guilt hollowed me out after that. I'd see her—Monica—my soon-to-be stepmom, standing with my dad. I know it's some messed up shit. I know I'm not supposed to fuck her, but I was barely a teenager. She didn't stop coming to my room, and I couldn't make her leave me alone. Avoiding her was the only thing that worked, but I had to go home eventually. Then, everything changed when Mom did something that no one expected and refused to divorce Dad. When Monica found out, she was livid. The sex changed after that.

I shove the thoughts away, forcing them to the back of my mind along with the guilt. She was the first of his lovers to go after me. Since then there have been more, and I did nothing to stop the rest of them. I learned quickly that they were all there for the money, for the lavish presents. We all got what we wanted, and no one knew what I was doing with my Dad's mistresses or what they did to me.

I want to keep it that way. It sounds horrible, and I know Luke is right. If Mom ever finds out, she'll kill me. Besides, it's not the kind of thing I like to talk about. I didn't want to be that kind of guy. It just happened.

My silence speaks volumes. Luke's hand rests on my shoulder before he walks out. "Start over, kid. Mistakes only pull you down as long as you hold onto them."

CHAPTER 7

CASSIE

"So, how'd your day go?" Robyn asks me later that night. She's still wearing her uniform from work, but she's pulled her silky hair into a ponytail and changed her shoes out for sparkly flip flops. We're standing in my aunt's kitchen making quesadillas.

I throw a tortilla in her face. Direct hit! Wahoo! The soft piece of food smacks the side of her face and then falls to the floor. "You suck, you know that?" She picks up the tortilla and laughs as she joins me at the counter. I'm shredding cheese and don't look up at her. My voice is clipped, irritated. "Do you introduce everyone that way or was it special, just for me?"

"Lighten up, Yankee." She grabs the avocados and starts to work on the guacamole. She tries to push some loose hairs back from her face without her hands, using her elbow. "He's hot and summer flings are fun. How was I supposed to know you're a goddamn nun? I hardly hear from you all year and then you show up on my doorstep. I thought, 'What would I like to do all summer if I were her?' Duh, Jonny Ferro."

"How do you even know him?" The Ferro family is filthy stinking rich, filled with brats that never get in trouble for anything. Everyone and their cat knows that family is bad news. "He's a freaking Ferro and we're in the middle of nowhere in Mississippi." I smack some cheese sauce and chicken onto another tortilla and stack it with the others.

"His family owns that huge-ass white house by the reservoir."

My hands still and I look at her. "Seriously?" It's gorgeous and all, but there's a glaring question. Why here? We're not anywhere near a major city. Jackson is over an hour away. This is the sticks with trees, trailers, and mansions scattered around a manmade lake.

She starts on the onions, dicing them into tiny pieces. "Yeah, they banished some crazy relative here a while back and holed him up in that place. The guy only leaves his house to hang out on his yacht, but Jonathan comes down once in a while. I caught him walking across the spillway one night and nearly ran him over with my car. The idiot was walking... can you even imagine?"

Okay, so walking across the spillway is stupid. Got it. Check. Still don't know why, but it appears that I'm not supposed to, so I don't ask. I'm still annoyed with her for dumping that guy on me. The rich brat is probably used to having girls fall all over him. That look in his eye, right before I left, had to be shock even though I thought it was something else. An uncomfortable twisting fills my stomach whenever I think about him, so I shove the guy out of my mind.

"Speaking of idiots," I say, changing the conversation, "did my brother happen to call?"

She shakes her head and tosses the chopped onion in the bowl with teary eyes. "Not that I know of. Aunt Paula doesn't have an answering machine—she thinks it's rude not to call every solicitor back—so it's hard to tell. Where's your cell phone anyway?"

"Mom took it away before she sent me down here." I bite my lip to stop talking.

"So, what'd you do?" Robyn stops working and looks over at me. "Come on, spill, Cassie."

"It's not what I did, it's what it looked like—and it embarrassed the crap out of her. I went to a graduation party for my friend and fell asleep in his bed. I didn't come home until dawn. Some kids took pictures of me sleeping on his bed and Grant climbed in and gave the thumbs up, like he nailed me." I make a face. "Everyone knows Grant's gay. He was just messing around. Short version, my mom saw one of the pictures and sent me down here to pull my act together."

Robyn is staring at me with dish plate eyes. "So, this is some sort of punishment?" I nod. "What about your Dad?"

"My mom was spitting bullets about it—what will the neighbors think," I mock her polite voice. Needless to say, Mom and I aren't BFFs. We barely manage to keep things cordial. Dad is the family glue, the peacekeeper, but he didn't stick his neck out for me this time. "Right before I left he came into my room and said some time away would be good for me." So here I am, staying with my Dad's little sister, a relative that I almost never see.

"Harsh." Robyn laughs and bumps her shoulder into mine as she mashes together the contents in the bowl. "Hey, wouldn't it be hysterical if you ended up in the papers for screwing Jon Ferro? Your mom would shit herself. There are worse things than having a snapshot of you in bed with a gay guy. She needs to get a little perspective."

I nod and smile tightly at her. My mom needs something, like a different daughter—one that is more like her perfect son. Toby is two years older than me and the perfect child. He's one of those guys that excels at everything and everyone loves him. I'm the opposite. I worked hard to get my grades. I still pulled A's, however since it wasn't without effort, it doesn't count for my mother. Toby is all smiles and confidence, where I'm shy and quiet—a wallflower, forever plain as my mom says.

Today was the first time that I didn't feel plain. The way Jonathan looked at me, well it was like I was worth looking at. I'm so positively average that no one glances my way twice, so when he did those things that should have gotten him slapped, I felt flattered. I'm such a head case.

My aunt works crazy hours to keep this little trailer. I guess the politically correct term is mobile home—or manufactured housing—I forget, but it's her house and she's been so nice to me since I walked off the plane. Robyn and I decided to make her dinner since she works late. We ran to the grocery store before coming home and have been getting dinner ready ever since. The conversation drifts all over the place, but Robyn brings it back around to sex.

"So," she says carefully, as she finishes setting the table. "What's with the no sex thing? Is that your Mom's idea—"

I cut her off. "No, it's my thing."

"Sorry, I didn't mean to pry, it's just that I don't know anyone who's proud to be a virgin and you seem to be, so I was wondering what I was missing. That's all.

Don't be all pissy at me for weeks. I won't be nosy again. Promise."

I glance up at her and smile. "You're such a dork."

"Shut up, virgin."

The tension between us is gone. I debate how much to tell her, because I want to say something. I know it sounds strange, but it makes sense to me. "At some point, I don't remember when," my voice wobbles a little because I remember exactly when I decided this, and the events around that day are trying to claw their way out of the box in the back of my head. I mentally shove them back down and continue with a smile on my face. "I decided that I wanted my first time to be on my wedding night. It's not religious or anything like that, I just liked the idea of being each other's first and only. It's romantic."

A male voice rings out behind me, "It's never going to happen."

Whirling around, I see Jonathan Ferro standing in the doorway to the kitchen. Dark jeans cling to his narrow hips as he leans against the jamb with his sculpted arms folded across his chest. His head is tipped to the side with that mess of dark hair falling into his eyes. My heartbeat races like someone is going to kill me. I stare at him with my mouth open, wondering why he's here.

"Hey, Jonny," Robyn says, as she crosses the kitchen to the sink.

"Hey, Rob. Your cousin here is really cute, but you need to get some things through her naïve little head before some big nasty boy crushes her heart." He pushes off the doorway and walks into the room without looking at me. I hate the way he talks about me like I'm invisible, like I'm a child that's too stupid to know better.

"It's not naïve," I counter, glaring at him.

"It is too." He reaches for the bowl on the table and pops an olive into his mouth before he rounds on me. Leaning back against the old beat up island, he says, "Think about it for a second, you're only interested in putting out for a guy that's never had a chick before? That's going to land you a gay guy or a liar. Every guy has had sex by the time he's our age. You're looking for a guy that doesn't exist." His cobalt eyes burn into mine. It feels like I've been scolded, slapped across the face.

"You're an asshole. Who invited you here anyway?" I sneer at him, clutching my fingers by my sides. He has no right to judge me. He doesn't even know me.

Grinning, he says, "Your aunt likes me." His hands move behind his back and he rocks on his toes. It's a juvenile gesture that's as clear as sticking out his tongue and *nah-nah-ing* me.

I take the bait. "And you'll lower yourself to schlep food from the dinner table inside a trailer? How kind of you."

"Cassie," my aunt's voice rings out behind me. Damn it. Why is everyone sneaking up on me today? "Mind your manners. Really." She hangs up her coat on a hook by the door. The floor creaks as she crosses the narrow room and heads for the kitchen.

I try to apologize but she just holds up her hand. "People live in different kinds of homes, Cassie. It's not the castle that makes the man, it's the heart. Kindhearted people can be kings or paupers." Her old gray eyes lock with mine. My Dad has those eyes and they do the same thing when he gives me that look.

My stomach grows cold and I nod. "Yes, Aunt Paula." I don't mean to, but I glance up at Jonathan. I expect to see a smug look on his face, but it isn't there. Instead, his eyes flash with concern and his lips are parted just enough to ask if I'm okay—after I acted like an asshole.

Robyn breaks the tension and slaps the hot dish down on the table. "Sit, eat. Stop arguing and act like a goddamn family."

Aunt Paula sighs, "Language, Robyn." Robyn pulls out Aunt Paula's chair and scoots her in.

"Sorry, I forgot. I haven't been out here in a while."

"You're welcome anytime Robyn." Aunt Paula smiles at my cousin who isn't really my cousin anymore. She's my ex-step-grandfather's wife's granddaughter. She's not blood, but she doesn't need to be. If something were horribly wrong, Robyn would be there in a blink. I can't even say that for my own mother.

Water is thicker than blood, at least that's true for me.

Aunt Paula's table is a small circle. We bump elbows, and normally I don't care, but Jonathan is on one side. I swear he's bumping me on purpose, first with his elbow and then with his knee. I take a bite of my dinner and look at him. "So freeloader, what are your summer plans?"

Jonathan grins. "You're my summer plans." He doesn't elaborate. Instead, he stuffs half a quesadilla into his mouth and chomps away.

Robyn gives me a lopsided smile. "You might have to make other arrangements Jonny-boy. My girl Cassie here seems to think that you're only after one thing."

Aunt Paula looks appalled. Her food falls to her plate as her jaw drops. "Robyn!"

Jonathan reaches out and pats my aunt's hand. "It's all right. I have a bad reputation, Ms. Barrett. Robyn is just looking out for your niece."

Aunt Paula eyes him and leans back in her chair. "So, out with it. What'd you do this time?"

Jonathan has a sheepish look on his face. "What makes you think I did anything? Maybe I just wanted to visit my uncle for the summer and have dinner with you fine ladies."

Aunt Paula shakes her head. "God bless your mother. You're a real handful."

Jonathan has no witty comeback, no quick retort. Instead, his eyes drop and he just nods. Someone has some serious mommy issues. I wonder what they are and if they're as screwed up as mine.

CHAPTER 8

JONATHAN

Those lips are burned into my mind. Dreams flutter behind my eyelids, making it impossible to sleep. Her impossibly sinful mouth, and the fact that Cassie seems to detest me, makes it hard to stop thinking about her. She's crazy, she has to be with notions like hers. I start to drift off again and see those perfect porcelain legs walking away from me. My mind replays the day again, always starting on Cassie and working backwards through the memories. Soft skin brushes against my lips as I kiss her cheek, and I inhale deeply. The light, sweet, scent she wore fills my head and makes me want her.

Mind wandering, I drift off picturing her next to me. Her face above mine, before she slowly sits up. Her clothes are gone and so is that irritating smile. Cassie looks down at me and slips her hand over my bare stomach, her perfect little fingers tracing each muscle. I watch her body as she breathes, happy to be near her. When she leans over, my pulse skyrockets. Her hair tickles my skin as her lips trail kisses down my chest, and past my waist. When her hot lips wrap around me, I can't control myself. I try to hold her, to give her what she wants, but the scene shifts and I know I'm dreaming.

I'm in my old room. The lights are out and the voice in my ear isn't Cassie's. It's hers—Monica's. "Does that feel good, baby?"

I dart upright, my heart racing too fast, with my body covered in sweat. What would've happened next is a fucking nightmare. My mind recognized it as soon as Monica's voice snaked through my mind. Pushing off the bed, I walk to the bathroom and splash water on my face.

When I head back to bed, I can't sleep. Guilt gnaws at me like it just happened. "Sex doesn't matter," I tell myself. It doesn't, it can't. It's something to do to pass the time. It means nothing and it never will.

After a second, I text Robyn. *U up?*

A few seconds later she writes back, *No.*

Your cousin hates me. I don't know why I'm telling her this. I just type whatever comes to mind. It's too late to be bothering her, and having written proof of anything is stupid, but it's Robyn. What's the worst she can do, show her cousin and Cassie laughs at me?

I hate u 2.

Ignoring her, I type, *Is she serious?*

About?

Did you really just ask me that? About the virgin thing. Telling a guy that she's holding onto her V-card, no you can't have it, and then gloating about it like virginity is something special—it's totally insane.

What do you want, Jonny?

What do I want? I want to nail your cousin. No, well, I do—but that's not the main thing. I need to know how she got there, why she's nearly twenty and actively refusing sex. It's insane. Doesn't she want it? How does she handle the urges? I picture Cassie with her hand down her panties and, oh fuck—that was a mistake.

Clearing my mind, I focus on why I'm bothering Robyn in the middle of the night. It's because she has something that I want. Then it hits me, *I want to know Cassie better. I want to know why she thinks the way she does.*

I think you're asking the wrong person.

I can't ask her. I don't even know her.

But you want to…?

I can picture Cassie's smile—the genuine one that she was wearing for a few seconds today. I want to put that look on her face. I want to know what makes her laugh, scowl, and grin. I want that version of her that I only saw when I shocked the hell out of her and her guard dropped for half a beat. *Yeah, I do.*

Go over there in the morning. Bring food. Don't leave when she tries to throw you out.

And…?

And get to know her, dumbass.

You're so eloquent when you're tired.

Fuck you. TTYL.

A vague plan forms in my mind and I smile. I wonder if it's really that simple. There's only one way to find out.

CHAPTER 9

CASSIE

It's 8:30am and someone is pounding on the metal screen door. It rattles like crazy until the hammering stops. I roll over and pull the blankets over my head. I planned on sleeping for another hour and there's no way in hell I'm opening the door. I'm pretty sure I'm in the 'hood part of the countryside with wild bears, rednecks with rifles, and stuff like that.

The knocking starts again. Moaning, I throw back the blankets and tug my hair away from my face and into a sloppy ponytail. I rub the sleep from my eyes and peer between the mini blinds in my room to look out at the front porch. Fuck. Is he serious? I glance down at my jammies and decide there is no way in hell that I am ever opening the door.

Just as I turn to go back to bed, Jonathan says, "I know you're there, so open the door. I have breakfast."

Padding down the narrow hall, I go to open the door with the idea that I'll chew him out and threaten to hit him in the head with a frying pan if he doesn't leave me alone. My heart thumps inside my chest as I reach for the knob. When I yank it back, I want to kill him. Jonathan looks perfect in his crisp cream T shirt and dark jeans, while I look like I just rolled out of bed. I don't unlock the screen door. Instead I fold my arms over my chest and stare at him through bits of rust. "Are you insane?"

"Probably." He smirks at me, and that smile sends a shiver through my body.

"And you think that's the best thing to say to get me to open the door?"

He waits a beat and then grins, saying, "I promise not to have sex with you."

"You're such an ass." I flick the lock on the screen and let him in. When Jonathan walks past me I get a whiff of his cologne. God he smells good. "Did you drown yourself in a vat of aftershave?"

He nods. "Just for you, baby. I figured, why make it easy for you to keep your hands off of me?"

"It doesn't make it harder, if that's what you think. I don't even like that cologne." Actually, I love that scent and I'm wondering how he found out. I may have to kill Robyn later.

Jonathan places two white bags down on the table and turns around and looks at me. "Eat your breakfast, crazy girl."

He slides a bag across to my seat, opposite him. It has everything from the McDonald's breakfast menu inside. My stomach grumbles at the scent of pancakes and grease. Yum. I pull out the food and dig in.

Jonathan watches me for a little bit before saying, "I've never met anyone like you."

"Likewise."

"It's refreshing. You're not trying to impress me and you seriously don't seem to care about my massive fortune. You haven't mentioned my brother killing his wife or asked where he buried the missing gun..." he smiles at me. "You didn't live in a cave or something before you came here, right? Or an asylum, maybe? You know what family I'm from, right?"

"Yes," I laugh and toss a piece of my pancake at him.

He's from the notorious Ferro family. They have too much money to know what to do with and the heir of the family fortune seems to be cursed. First, Sean, the eldest was the heir, and there was that whole mess with his wife. I'm not sure if he killed her or not. Just because someone doesn't cry it doesn't mean they're guilty. The media played up how stoic Sean had been at the time, like it automatically made him a murderer. Then, control of the fortune was passed to the middle brother, Peter. He had something horrible happen and has been mostly off the map. Then there's Jonathan, the youngest and newest heir. The things I've heard about him don't line up with this sock with sandal wearing guy. Maybe the press just makes crap up. Another story, another dollar, another day. Yes, I'm jaded. So sue me.

Jonathan picks at his hash browns for a second. When he glances up, he hits me with those vulnerable baby blues. "Then why?"

"Why what?" I'm not following him, like at all. I kind of wish I was. That look is intoxicating and as I gaze at him, I realize I never want it to end. I'm insane. I blink and look away, then take another bite of food, intentionally stuffing my mouth to look as unattractive as possible.

Jonathan's eyes wander around the little kitchen. He takes a bite of food, chews, and sits back in his chair. "Why the instant disdain? You don't like me, but it seems to have nothing to do with my garish amount of cash, or my last name—so then what is it?"

My words are harsh, but the smile on my face and my sarcastic tone lightens the punch. "You ever think it might just be you?"

The corners of his lips tip up. "Of course not, everyone loves me."

"*Everyone* is not the correct word."

Jonathan glances up and gives me a look that makes my knees weak. "It will be."

CHAPTER 10

JONATHAN

Cassie doesn't let her defenses drop when I'm around. That light laugh and shy smile only come out when Robyn is with us. It drives me insane. It's like she's shut me out on purpose, like she doesn't want to have anything to do with me. Robyn picked a movie last night and we all went. Cassie ended up next to me and she sat there, leaning as far away as possible, stiff as a board. There have been a few occasions where she seems to relax. I love those times. I crave them and I go over to her house every day to try again.

This isn't like me. Normally, whatever I want falls into my lap, but it'll be a goddamn miracle if that happens. Cassie on my lap would make me smile for the rest of the summer. No, I'm not that shallow. This isn't about the quest—it's about the girl. She makes me feel things I've never felt, and want things that I can't have. Everything seems better when she's around, less dismal. Because let's face the facts, no one cares if a rich guy is depressed. No one gets how isolated it is, and how skewed things get. Never knowing who really likes you and who's using you really fucks with the mind. At some point, everything became fake—even me—but Cassie lured me out. I want to be myself around her, so I try harder.

Handing Cassie the bag of food, I sit down at her aunt's little table. "So, what are we going to do today?" To date, I haven't been able to get her to go anywhere with me. Well, not really. We took a walk once, but as soon as we hit the end of the road that led to the spillway, she refused to take another step. I told her that it's perfectly safe, I even walked over the damn thing once before. Instead of following me toward the bridge over the water, she just burst out laughing.

Today, I'm not taking no for an answer.

"Go somewhere?" Cassie glances over the top of the white bag and arches an eyebrow. "We? As in me and you?"

"Yeah, that's what 'we' means." I lean my elbow on the table and give her a goofy grin.

"Yeah, I don't think so." She takes a fork full of pancake and stuffs it in her mouth.

Sometimes I think she's taking bigger bites to gross me out, but it's a turn-on seeing her mouth open wide, and then watching the food slip over those perfect lips. I've lost my mind. I feel it slipping away from me. No sex in a month and I can't think. Whoever said sex gunks up the works wasn't getting any. My brain worked fine when I was screwing around. This starvation diet is making me mental, but it's self-inflicted. I don't want anyone else. I want her.

I'm staring at her, my eyes locked on her mouth as she chews. "What?" Cassie spews pancake crumbs and grins.

"You're trying to gross me out. Come on, Cassie. I'm not that bad. Give me a chance."

"A chance to do what?" The smile falls off her face as her gaze lowers. A fork full of pancake lingers as she speaks. "There's no scenario in which you and I are anything more than friends."

"So, what's wrong with that?"

Her face lifts and she looks at me. There's a confusion in those dark eyes. "You want to be friends?"

"Yeah, why not?"

Cupping a hand to her ear, she says, "What was that? I think I heard you wrong. Because it sounded like Mr. Love 'Em and Leave 'Em wants to be friends." She laughs, still thinking I'm kidding. Her eyes fall to her plate and when she looks up again, the smile drops. Her voice changes. It's that light uncertain tone she uses with Robyn. "Are you serious?"

I want to claw my way across the table and take her in my arms, but if this is the best I can hope for, I want it. Friends. Glancing down at the table, I intentionally avoid her eyes and pick at my food. "We know each other's biggest secrets. It seems like the start of a friendship to me. Besides, what else are you going to do all summer? Sit here and wait for Robyn to get home?"

My heart is thumping way too fast for something like this. I'm not nailing her, so I don't get why my pulse races when she's around. Hot girls don't get me into this state, so it's something else. My eyes sweep over her face as she gazes at me, considering my words like they're grand jury testimony. "Do you act like this with everyone, Cassie? Is it so hard to be your friend?"

Her smile turns into a smirk. "I don't know. Do you invite yourself over to everyone's house, or just mine?" The corners of her mouth twitch, like she enjoys flirting with me.

"Just yours. There's a recluse that lives here, you know. She refuses to go outside and has the pasty skin to prove it. And I mean pale, like she'd get lost in the snow, albino, kind of pale. Snowball city."

Cassie scowls and folds her arms over her chest, thrusting her breasts higher as she does it. Do women do that on purpose? You can't jack up your boobs and then yell at us for looking. It's like pointing at them and saying 'don't look.'

I lean back in my chair, and kick my legs out under the table, trying damn hard not to look at those perfect tits. I need a distraction. My foot bumps hers and I grin, until Cassie kicks my shin, hard. "Hey!" I sit up.

Grinning ear to ear, Cassie stands and grabs her trash. "Snowball, my ass."

I stand and follow her to the garbage can. After she throws her stuff in, Cassie turns suddenly, not realizing that I'm right behind her. She gasps and her shoulders tense, like I'm too close. Leaning nearer to her face, I give her my most charming crooked smile. "You did not just invite me to look at your ass."

She laughs, like, actually laughs. "You're such a…" She inhales deeply, slowly, and tilts her head to the side as her lungs fill with air. Dark curls fall over one shoulder before her gaze lowers for half a second. When she glances back up at me, the unthinkable happens. "So, where are we going?"

Blinking like I've been hit in the head with a two by four, I follow her body with my eyes as she slips past me. "I'm sorry, did you agree to go out with me?" I toss my stuff in the trash and turn around, watching that perfect smile light up her face. It's flawlessly girlish, but somehow she makes it sexy at the same time. The woman is a walking oxymoron.

"I agreed to go somewhere with you— as friends." Her body language shifts and the confidence slips away. Her shoulders hunch forward a little bit and her eyes fall to the floor, skittering around, landing anywhere but on me. "Not as—"

"Not as what, Cassie?"

She blushes and doesn't look up. A quick smile covers her face to hide her reaction, before she tucks her hair behind her ear. I step closer to her, way too close for the kind of friend she wants me to be. I can't stop staring at her, drinking in that smooth skin and those dark lashes. Cassie won't look up, which kills me, because if she did, I could lean in and kiss her.

Heart slamming into my ribs, I steady my voice and lean in close to her ear.

"Come on, pasty chick. Let's get you some sunshine."

———

When Cassie steps outside, she sees the little black sports car, and hesitates. Before she can run back inside, I grab her wrist and pull her after me. "You can't back out now. Come on. Luke has a boat, or we can just hang out on the dock. Whatever you want, but you can't hide inside all summer."

Cassie grips her wrist after I drop it and walks to the car. I don't open her door, even though I want to. She'll take it the wrong way. When she slips in next to me, I start the engine and pull out of the gravel driveway. As I talk, I see the fingers on her right hand lift, like she's thinking about opening the door.

"Afraid?" I smirk at her, before returning my eyes to the road.

"No," she says, like it's ridiculous, as if she has no reason to be nervous around me—but she clearly is.

Laughing, I bait her, "Yes, you are. Your hand is getting ready to pull the door open and jump out. Seriously, Cassie. What kind of mental are you?"

She sneers at me and drops her hand to her lap. "What kind of mental am I? What about you? You invite yourself over every day and pester the hell out of someone who wants nothing to do with you. And you think I'm mental." She folds her arms over her chest and stares out the window, muttering.

"Come on, now. Just admit it—you like me." I grin at her, but she doesn't look my way. "I get your panties in a bunch and you have no idea what to do about it, because I'm not the guy you're looking for." I'm playing with fire here, and damn well aware of the consequences if I verbally torch her by mistake, but I can't stand it when she's tense. It turns me into a neurotic mess.

Her jaw drops open and she turns in slow motion with wide eyes. "My panties are not in a bunch." Her jaw locks as she glares at me.

I grip the steering wheel tighter, and run into the no-fly zone like an escaped inmate. "No? Did you forget to wear them?

Commando isn't something I would have thought you'd be into." The smile on my face increases as Cassie's gaze narrows. Come on Cass, laugh. Slap me and laugh.

She makes a strangled sound in the back of her throat, as she crushes the air like a madman with her hands. "You are so…!"

"Adorable? Sexy? Swoon worthy?" Her lips purse together and she gives me a look that says I'm losing her. Quickly, I add, "And totally into you, by the way." That does it. The tension breaks like a dam and flows away. She turns that beautiful face toward me. Her lips are parted slightly, like she doesn't know what to say. I prattle on, egging her, baiting her, hoping to God that she bites. "It's probably because you hate my guts, but the way you treat me is refreshing. I just can't get enough."

"I don't hate you." She tucks her chin and grins, glancing at me out of the corner of her eye. This is news to me. A wicked grin spreads across her face. It soaks in and makes her eyes sparkle like gems. "I loathe you and your charm, and your annoyingly attractive face."

"I'm annoying?"

"Very."

"Wait, did you say attractive? And are we talking devastatingly annoying, or more of a totally do-able kind of annoying? Annoying's code for hot, right?" I flash her a smile as I turn into the driveway at Uncle Luke's. She laughs and smacks my arm, leaning closer to me for half a second. The sound is amazing, completely perfect, and exactly what I wanted.

CHAPTER 11

CASSIE

A few weeks pass. I'm up and dressed by the time Jon comes looking for me every morning. I have no intention of doing anything with him, but he is hot and I don't want to look like a slob when he's around. Besides, there's no way he's 'the one.' Jonathan has dipped his stick into too many places and the thought is utterly unappealing. Okay, maybe not utterly, and maybe not late at night when my mind wanders, but I want the guy to be my first and vice versa. Jonathan's the opposite of what I'm looking for, but he helps me kill time and I find myself smiling more and more. I know it has something to do with him, but I'd rather not think about it.

Either way, I'm grateful for the time away from home. I grew up in North Babylon, right off of Deer Park Avenue. I'm used to nonstop noise at all hours and an endless array of things to do, so many things that I never had time to think about what I really like. Life has a faster pace up there. In some ways that's awesome. Getting lunch at a drive through in less than a minute is spectacular. And missed. No one is in a hurry down here. It's like they have all the time in the world. Slowing down and not strangling the McDonald's lady has become one of my missions. I can be patient. Maybe. Okay, I suck at it, but I'm trying. If Jon can do it, I can. He's had the same hurried life, always moving forward, frantically so at times.

I'm just glad for the change in pace and to have some space from my mom. Think of the most uptight, critical woman you can imagine—now combine that chick with a saintly church going woman and that's my mother. Everyone thinks she's great and she is wonderful to everyone, except me. They all get this pristine version of mom that doesn't exist behind closed doors.

I get the over-critical edition, who's constantly putting me down, correcting me, and making so many passive aggressive jabs that I seriously think she hates me. It's gotten to the point that I can barely tolerate being in the same room as Mom. Everything I do is wrong or not good enough. Every accomplishment that puts a smile on my lips only makes her frown, like I could have done so much better. Academically, I'm at the top of my class. Only one person beat me, so now she treats me like I'm dumb too—as if being salutatorian is the equivalent of being the class idiot. For her, that's what it meant— failure. I'm not number one, I'm number two and she treats me like the piece of shit she thinks I am.

My friends don't see it. She hides that part of herself and saves it just for me. They think the slope of my shoulders and my downturned face is from some teenage crap, but it's not. It's from her. The woman ruthlessly picks at me like a vulture—from dawn 'til dusk—criticizing everything from my clothes to my mind to my lack of a flat belly. I'm not fat, but my stomach isn't ever going to be perfectly hard and smooth no matter how many crunches I do—and that's not good enough. Not for my dear mother who wants the perfect daughter at all cost. My life is filled with verbal lashings and it's just so good to be around someone who likes me the way I am.

Jonathan seems to enjoy my company just as much as I'm enjoying his. Although there's this easy way about him, I know there's a wall between us. Secrets, failures, and insecurities erected it, and it towers over us. I don't know what his story is, but it seems like his ego is as fragile as mine. He overcompensates in the same ways, throwing barbed words out when I say something that hits too close to home—just like I do. I know that play and have done the same thing too many times to count. I wonder what he's hiding behind those beautiful blue eyes and the fake smile that's always plastered across his face.

And that's when things take an unexpected turn. We're in a middle state, where we are sort of friends, but still cautious of one another. We eat breakfast and then find something to do until Robyn gets off work. The three of us make dinner and hang out until Aunt Paula comes home. It's easy and feels normal even though it's totally weird if you stop and think about it.

I mean, there's a billionaire hanging out in a trailer because he wants to.

We're sitting at Aunt Paula's little table eating breakfast. The house is completely quiet, which makes my chewing sound horsey-loud. It's very sexy. I try to quiet my chomping, but it's no use.

Jonathan looks up at me and smiles. "I don't care how loud you chew. You're parents really messed you up, you know that?"

I avert my eyes, chomp quickly, and swallow my food. We know each other a little better now. Months of breakfast together will do that. It's impossible not to talk about my neurotic thoughts when half of them were inflicted by my mother. "Me? What about you? What'd you do that they banished you down here, anyway?"

Jonathan's smile fades slightly, before it resumes at full blast. If I hadn't been watching him, I wouldn't have noticed. Whatever he did to get himself sent down here was major. I looked through the papers to try and figure out what he could have possibly done, but there was nothing.

His mother must have taken care of it before it hit the press.

"So," Jonathan shoves the last of his egg sandwich in his mouth, and says, "this art exhibit is opening soon, and I have an in with the curator. We can look at the exhibition before everyone else, while they finish setting it up. You want to go?"

"Nice dodge. Very subtle." I watch him for a second, wondering if he ever drops that damn mask he's wearing. It's always there—a perfect smile on a perfect face—guarding his thoughts like a German Shepard.

I lean back in my chair and ask, "So, you like art?" I'm surprised. I probably shouldn't be, but I am. Picturing Jonathan playing football and liking things that are fast and fun is easier. Art isn't like that. It's pensive and pure.

Nodding, he leans back in his chair. "Yeah, and you shouldn't sound surprised. Rich people like art, remember?"

I have trouble imagining him in a mansion, especially since I keep seeing him in an old mobile home. Smiling, I reply,

"Okay, so where is this show and whose is it?"

"Ah, that's a surprise, but we do have to haul ass and look sort of presentable." He glances at my cut-offs and my tank top.

"I get it. You want me to change."

"It's an art show, babe, not a barbeque."

"Ha ha. Give me a few minutes. I'll be right back." Before I forget, I turn abruptly and lightly smack the back of his head. "And stop calling me babe."

He chuckles as I run down the dark, narrow hall to my room and dig through my clothes looking for a dress. I brought a church dress, in case Aunt Paula wanted to go, and a clubbing dress in case Robyn wanted to be adventurous one night. Neither is quite right. It's possible that I can make do and tone down the clubbing dress. The neckline is a little low and the fabric is clingy, but the skirt flares out just above the knee and makes my legs look nice. The problem is the neckline, it's a cleavagefest. I need a wrap or something to tone it down.

I holler to Jonathan that I'm almost ready and duck into Aunt Paula's room.

We're about the same size, so I dig through her closet looking for something that will work. A fuzzy black sweater catches my eye. It's perfect, at least I think it is until I pull it on. It's cut short and ends at my waist with little cap sleeves, however the fuzz makes it look like a Muppet was slaughtered and laid across my shoulders.

Jonathan's voice comes from the doorway. "I think emo Elmo has seen better days."

When I turn to look at him, the corners of his lips twitch, like he's trying not to laugh. I stare at my reflection and hear every nasty word my mother's ever said to me about my figure. They crash into me like a tidal wave. Even though I'm looking at my reflection, I no longer see myself, and the smile fades from my lips.

Jonathan's voice is suddenly right behind me, very close to my ear. "You don't need this. It's too hot and you look perfect without it." His fingers touch my shoulders lightly, making me jump. I can't help it. It feels like I've fallen off the top of the staircase and landed flat on my back.

There's no air and my lungs won't work. What the hell is wrong with me?

Jonathan raises his hands and steps back. "I'm sorry, I didn't mean to—"

Smiling too brightly, I spin on my heel. "No, it's fine. You just startled me, that's all." My eyes drift up to his and our gazes hold like that for a moment. I look away and pick at the sweater. It takes way too much effort to take it off, but I manage. Without the damn thing, I feel naked. It doesn't hide any of my body flaws, and the way this dress bodice clings all the way down to my hips shows off every imperfection I have. Before the sweater is dropped on Aunt Paula's bed, I stare down at it. I need it. Every piece of me is screaming to put it back on.

Then Jonathan's fingers are around mine, preventing me from putting the sweater back on. He's a step away from me, but I can still feel his breath on the side of my face when he speaks. "You look beautiful without it."

I don't believe him. I need it. A half grin covers my face when I feel a retort die in my throat. Jonathan places his finger under my chin and lifts my eyes to meet his. "You have no idea how gorgeous you are, do you?"

I laugh like he's joking, but that just makes Jonathan's brows pinch together, like he can't fathom that I don't know what I look like—but I do know. I see myself every morning. I see my out of control hair, my over-sized hips, my unfashionably pale skin, and normal-sized breasts. I'm nothing to look at, and I'm okay with that. I know what I am, but the way he looks at me almost makes me believe him.

"You're pretty enough for both of us." I turn away from him, severing the contact. My heart races faster, like I'm being chased by a flock of rabid bunnies.

Somehow he took hold of the sweater and doesn't offer it back. My arms don't know where to go, so they fold across my chest. Jonathan says softly, "I'm serious, Cassie. What happened to you? Can you really not see it? When we walk around together, all the guys check you out. You're hot. You have to know—"

I swat my hand at him, meaning to dismiss his words that are bringing me close to tears for no explicable reason. "Everyone is looking at you. You're a Ferro, Jonathan. I'm not. They're looking at you and if a few eyes fall my way, it's curiosity and nothing more."

My arms are tightly nestled against my chest when Jonathan slips his finger over my hands and works them into the center of my palm. He slips one hand away and then the other, uncrossing my arms. He smiles at me sadly, like he knows how damaged I am—like he's never met expectation either. "Come on, Hale." His voice is kind, encouraging. He turns and keeps a hold on my hand for a second too long, pulling me towards the doorway before he lets go.

I glance back at the sweater on the bed, and leave it behind.

CHAPTER 12

CASSIE

"What the hell is this?" I stop dead in my tracks after fighting to shut the front door of the trailer. The metal by the lock is bent like someone hit it with a bat a few years ago. It takes two hands to close and lock the thing, which is why I failed to notice the sleek black SUV at the curb, complete with driver.

Jonathan glances back at me. "Our ride. Come on."

I stop on the rickety little porch. "I can't—"

"Yes, you can." Jonathan turns back and looks at me.

A million thoughts smash into each other like atoms in a reactor when I see the car. It confirms exactly who Jonathan Ferro is, and it obviously links us if the press sees us together in this car. For the first time, I really see who I'm with and I don't know what to do. He's not a normal guy—he never was.

With a dramatic sigh, Jonathan steps up in front of me. The tiny deck is too small for both of us at the same time. He's too close, nose to nose. My stomach flutters when I catch his gaze. The intensity of that look is enough to floor me. My breath catches in my throat and I'm wondering what he's going to do.

Jon's voice is low, barely a whisper. "Walk to the car and get in like a normal person."

"You're not a normal person." My voice quivers as I glance over his shoulder and see the driver step out and open the door to the backseat.

"That's where you're wrong. I'm quite normal, actually. In fact, I'm so normal that I'll do what any man would do if you don't walk there yourself." His eyes are brilliant, sparkling with mirth and determination. It makes my stomach dip like I'm in a free fall.

My voice catches in my throat, "And what's that?"

"Throw you over my shoulder and carry you." He grins at me as my eyes increase to the size of tennis balls.

"You wouldn't!"

"Try me."

My pulse rushes in my ears as we stare each other down. The idea of having his hands on me is too much. I cave and go to push past him, but Jonathan won't move. When I glance up into his face, he's looking down at me. There's no gleam in his eyes, no smirk on his lips. His lashes are lowered as he gazes at my mouth. There's barely any space between us and it's difficult to resist the urge to slip my hands around his waist and hold him. I'm drawn to him. I know it and I've accepted it. My plan to not act on the attraction has been going well. Right up until this moment. The way my heart flutters and toes curl in my heels is too much. I imagine him closing the space between us, I want him to, but—

The thought cuts off, because Jonathan leans in slowly. Panic sets a fire in my mind and everything turns to chaos. My reasons, my organized thoughts of why we can't be together, go up in smoke. I have half a second to decide before those soft, pale, pink lips meet mine. Every inch of me is screaming to lean into him, to let him kiss me, but I can't. I can't. I've waited too long looking for the right guy to throw it away now. My kiss doesn't belong to Jonathan.

He can't have it.

The thoughts rush through my mind like spilling water. Before I know it, I'm plastered against the screen door, sucking in air, trying to get some space between us. Jonathan slows when he notices my reaction, pressing his lips together as he watches me try to merge with metal. My face turns to the side and I look down. Heart beating hard, I say, "I can't. Please don't."

He watches me for a moment. "Not even a kiss?"

I shake my head and don't look up at him. I don't trust myself, and I saved this kiss for so long. It's not his. "No, I'm sorry."

He steps back and nearly falls off the porch, which makes me look up and react. I reach out for him and grab his wrist, steadying him as he steps onto the ground.

He glances at my hand for a second and then up into my face. "Thanks." He pulls his wrist away and takes a shaky breath, pushing the hair out of his face and trailing his hands down his neck when he's done. "Damn, I haven't been this inept in a while… I thought—"

I shake my head, not wanting him to apologize. "It's weird, I know—"

"It's not weird at all." He looks up at me and I can tell he means it. "You have more conviction in that one belief than I have in my whole body. So, no first kiss?"

I shake my head as my face flames red and avert my eyes. "Not yet. I'm saving it."

He nods and looks down at his hands before shoving them in his pockets. "Then I'll be certain not to screw that up for you. I just wanted you to know—without a shadow of doubt—how beautiful and completely kissable you are…" His voice trails off like he doesn't know what else to say.

I glance up at him from under my lashes, careful not to meet his gaze, and smile. I can't help it. Awkward silence starts building and quickly grows bigger. I hate it and smash it back with some classic Cassie. I stomp down the steps and walk up to him. "I'd kiss you if I wasn't waiting."

He smirks. "So, you're eighteen and never been kissed?" I nod. A wicked grin crosses his face and I can't tell if he's serious or joking. "Promise me something. When you turn thirty—if Mr. Right still hasn't swept you off your feet—come and find me."

My stomach twists hard. The way he looks at me makes me think he isn't talking about lips on lips, but something more. I swallow hard and nod, tucking a curl behind my ear. "Don't worry, when I give up, you'll be the guy I go looking for to deflower me."

Jonathan nearly chokes at my comment, and then we both start laughing. It pushes things back to the way they had been, which is good. I spend my entire day with him, every day. Jonathan's become the reason I get out of bed in the morning and has learned more about me than most of my friends at home. I hold everyone at arm's length, but this guy managed to get closer. It makes me wonder when I dropped my guard, and if he snuck under the fence or if I let him in.

CHAPTER 13

JONATHAN

Jonathan Gray is a famous painter that I've been following for a few years. I made the mistake of buying one of his pieces a few years ago and giving it to my mother as a gift. She has no appreciation of art, other than the hope that it'll increase in value. When I bought it, Jonathan Gray was a no-name, just another hack slapping paint on a canvas, as mother kindly stated.

A few weeks later the guy became huge, like instantly famous. Mom didn't care. Suddenly my good eye was perceived as luck. Even an idiot can get lucky. That's what my family thinks of me, that I have no mind and that I'm all about flash and charm, with nothing deeper.

After a while it's easier to give in and be what they see instead of trying to convince them that they're wrong. I admit it, I gave up. I'm the monster they made me into. Serious about nothing, and a total player.

The past few weeks here have been different though. Something about Cassie is different. She seems to see through me. It's like she knows there's something else beneath this smokescreen I'm wearing all the time. It's like she knows I'm a fake and is okay with it. It's hard to explain, but when someone actually sees the person inside and doesn't run screaming, or try to get into my pants, I don't know what to make of it.

On the car ride over, Cassie is quiet. I bump my shoulder into hers. "When we first met, you asked me what I did that got me banished here for the summer."

She smiles at me. "You don't have to say anything, Jon. It's none of my business. I shouldn't have asked."

I press my lips together for a second, as my hands get hotter. This could backfire, but I want her to know. A lot has happened in a short time, and it feels like things should go this way. If there are walls between us, I don't want them there because of me. I glance at the driver. The divider is up so I know he can't hear. "I don't mind that you asked. Actually, you're the only person who did ask. Everyone else just assumes that I did the same old shit and pissed off my mother, but it wasn't like that. There's this school in Jersey that is doing some pretty cool things. They have this curriculum that favors kinetic learning and incorporates computers, online programs, and some other stuff that puts it light-years ahead of every other school in the country. It's impressive." I feel her gaze on the side of my face as I speak. Damn, my palms are hot. I don't look at her. I continue and spit it out as fast as I can. "So I bought it."

"You bought a public school?"

"A private school, actually. A very expensive private school. I didn't tell anyone, I just did it." I smile foolishly and glance over at her. "The reason I found out about it in the first place was because this hot girl was failing Chem. She was telling me about it, and I kind of told her that I'd fix it. She offered her gratitude and my mother caught us." I feel like an ass telling her that I slept with someone else, but that was the catalyst this time and I don't want to lie to her.

Continuing, I say, "Mom threw my ass on a plane before I could explain. I wanted the school because I want to make things better. I think the school system is fucked up, but it has so much potential, and this one place is doing it right. I wanted to run studies on their model and see what it would take to utilize it, but no one cares about that part. They basically thought it was a really roundabout way to buy a good time. My mom covered it up. No one knows." I don't look over at her, and I can't stand the thought of seeing the judgment in her eyes.

It's deafeningly quiet for a moment, then Cassie says, "I didn't know you cared about education. First I find out you like art, and now this." She bumps my shoulder and smiles up at me.

My stomach twists and I realize her approval matters to me. I wonder if she knows that little story will get me skinned alive if anyone finds out. My lips twist up, but it's a nervous grin that comes out lopsided. "Don't tell anyone." I wink at her and clear my throat, cautiously avoiding her eyes. "They'll think there's more to me than a pretty face and killer abs."

"Whoever thinks you're all looks is a little low in the smart department. I knew you were more than looks the first day we met."

"Really?"

"Yes, really." She shakes her head slightly, making that silky, dark hair fall over her shoulder.

God, I wish I could have kissed her. I roll the words around on my tongue before spitting them out. It sounds like a confession, one I don't really want to talk about. "No one really notices that about me." My voice drops to a whisper as I stare out the window.

She touches my arm and I look over at her. Her words are careful. I see it in her eyes when she speaks. "Do you give them a chance to notice? I mean, you're all flash and don't really let anyone see more than that, do you?"

"I let you see the rest." I glance up at her, meeting her big brown eyes full on, wishing that I had a chance with her. If I could go back and change everything, I would.

"And how's that working out?" She tips her head to the side and studies me.

"The verdict isn't in yet, but right now it's pretty nice." Cassie treats me to one of those rare smiles, the kind that makes my heart flip, and she shyly looks away.

CHAPTER 14

CASSIE

Jon was so serious in the car. For a second, it felt like he wasn't pretending anymore. The walls came down, and he was just a guy. I didn't like it, I loved it. If he acted like that all the time, I'd be screwed. There's no way I could let him walk out of my life. Thank God Jonathan reverted back into the arrogant edition as soon as we stepped out of the car.

Heading across the parking lot, he takes my hand and pulls me past a mob of people. "What's going on?"

"Nothing. This guy always has protesters. Let's head inside and get the sneak peak tour. There'll be a few other patrons there that have purchased from Gray in the past, but other than that—we'll have the floor to ourselves. Pretty cool, right?"

He holds the door open for me and we duck inside. "You're proud of yourself."

"Just a little bit."

We're taken to the exhibit after Jonathan introduces himself to the director. Canvases that are taller than I am line the walls, each one somber and mute. Women are depicted in paint, their expressions a little too sexual for me to look at with Jon standing next to me.

When did he become Jon? I wonder. I glance at him out of the corner of my eye, watching him wander over to a painting with his hand on his chin. He stares at it, unblinking, unafraid that anyone is watching him. The subject matter makes me blush. The woman on the canvas looks like she's in ecstasy, but she's alone. Between her isolation and the colors, it feels sad— lost almost.

Jon turns to me, his arm folded over his chest with his other tapping his jaw. "So, what do you think of the infamous Jonathan Gray?"

I shrug, and try not to look at Jon. The paintings are more evocative than I thought, so I joke, knowing damn well that it's a defense mechanism. "So, what's wrong with this guy?" I tilt my head to the side and look at yet another painting of a naked woman. The monochromatic tones are so somber it makes me want to cry.

Jon moves next to me and slips his hands into his pockets. "Yeah, I think they all feel sad too. I don't know. I'd be seriously happy if I had this chick posing for me at my house."

I glance at him out of the corner of my eye and smirk. "I'm surprised you haven't. It says the artist and models are from New York."

Jonathan fake laughs and steps in front of me, blocking the view of the painting. Folding his arms over his chest, he says, "I haven't screwed every woman in New York."

"No, I know. You spread your seed abundantly over the Tri-State area. Can't forget Connecticut. They get pissy when we do that." I smirk at him and walk over to another painting, glancing out the window as I pass. There are people gathered outside with poster boards that have thick black letters sprawled across each one. They seem agitated, as if something changed down there.

Jonathan laughs deeply and shakes his head. He trails behind me, stopping in front of the window. "Damn, they're getting noisy out there."

"I'm surprised they let us in with all that going on outside."

He shrugs, "I'm not. It's the only perk of being a Ferro."

"Yeah, that and obscene amounts of money." Glancing over my shoulder, I flash him a grin.

Jonathan has this way about him, like nothing I can say will ever get to him. Every compliment or burn I've thrown his way just rolls off his shoulders like his skin is made of Kevlar. Nothing gets to his heart—ever. It makes me wonder what happened to him, what made him this way.

Jonathan steps away and looks at his shoe before standing next to me. The painting in front of us is pale skin on snow, cream and white, and haunted eyes that make me shiver. I stare at the canvas way too long with him by my side, and ask, "What do you think his deal is?"

"I think that's a chick, Cassie. I mean, those could be man boobs, but her ass is a little too—" I jab him in the side with my elbow and render him silent as he chortles.

"No, you dork. I mean the artist— Jonathan Gray. What's wrong with him? All these paintings look so sad. It's like staring into an emotional void and the woman is insignificant."

A single brow lifts on his face, like Jon's impressed. His arms fold over his toned chest as he tucks his chin in. His lips press together and part, like he wants to say something, but he doesn't.

My voice is soft, "Tell me. I know you're thinking something—just say it. It can't possibly make my opinion of you any worse," I tease. He laughs once, but still says nothing. I copy his stance and tip my head up. Eyeing him, I say, "Your silence makes me think that you must be contemplating boning the subject."

Jonathan laughs way too loudly, making a few people, including a security guard, look our way. A sweet smile plays across his face before his flush fades. Damn, he's cute.

"God, you're crass. Although the formal language made it sound much more refined. Thank you, I appreciate that."

"Any time." I smirk and look positively smug, until he starts talking.

Jonathan's eyes don't wander back my way, instead he stares at the painting like he's lost in a dream. "There was this woman back when I was a kid—barely a teenager—she looked like this. Everything about her was soft and alluring. It felt like she was heaven, a safe place in a storm." He presses his lips together and swallows hard. "But some storms never end. They go on and on and the turmoil builds to a fucking froth and this is what you get." He gestures to the painting. "The haunted eyes and the woman in the mist fade to white, but she's never gone—her betrayal is always there, smack in front of my goddamn face." For a moment neither of us says anything, but then he glances over at me. "Too much for you?"

"Not at all. Everyone has a dark side, Jon." I watch him for a second. He's breathing hard and won't look at me. "Hey, real friends don't run when things get bad. I don't know who that woman was or what she did to you, but—"

"She was great. She didn't do anything any thirteen year old guy wouldn't love to do, but—" he shakes his head and pushes his hair back.

"But what?" What the hell is he talking about?

He looks straight into my eyes and it feels like every breath of air has been sucked from the room. The people who were standing so close flitter away. The security guard becomes a gray blob to my right and the elderly couple on the bench fades away. In that moment, everything is him.

When his gaze meets mine, it's as if his blue eyes are waves and he's drowning. I can see he's in peril, but it's too late. This storm has already passed and it drowned him. The man standing before me is a carcass of what he was, an illusion covered in pretty smiles and smooth words. Even though we haven't known each other that long, I see through him.

The vulnerability in that moment makes my anger flare to life. I hate it. I hate that someone hurt him. I hate that I've been trampled over and over again and did nothing to stop it. I hate that I'm weak and that he's hurting. I don't want him to hurt, not now. Not ever. If I lift my hand and touch him, the moment will crumble into a million pieces, but the urge to hold him in my arms is overtaking me.

My fingers brush the back of his hand gently and he shivers. He blinks rapidly and the pleasant expression he wears like a mask slips back into place. "But I shouldn't complain. I mean, I have no reason to…" His eyes look everywhere, except at me.

"It's not complaining."

He clears his throat and shifts his shoulders, tightening his folded arms. "You don't talk about your mother, and I won't talk about mine."

Uh, yes I do. But, I don't understand. My brain sorts through the things he just told me—which sounded sexual—until he mentions his mother. Shaking my head, I ask, "Your mother? What does she—"

He's so uncomfortable, squirming in front of me like I'm going to stomp him with my shoe. He's like a bug on its back, unable to recover without a little help. I smile and look away, tucking my hair behind my ear as I do so. The old security guard in front of me is touching the wedding band on his left hand. His body is tense, but I don't know why.

That's when the unthinkable happens. The floor starts to shake and before I know what's happening a loud sound comes from across the room. Shrapnel flies at us, and before I can blink Jonathan grabs hold of me and tackles me to the floor. He rolls us under a bench on the far side of the room. Shots are fired, but there's so much smoke that I can't see anything. I claw at Jonathan and bury my face in his shoulder, shaking.

Holding me tight, we stay like that under the bench. It seems like years, but it's only seconds. Terror courses through my veins as his body remains wrapped around mine. He speaks to me, but I can't hear him. My ears are still ringing with the deafening silence that followed the blast. I keep my face buried in his chest with my heart pounding so violently that I'm sure he can feel it. The smoke starts to clear and

Jonathan says something, but I don't know what. The ringing won't stop.

Crying, I shake my head and say, "No, Jon. Don't leave me." I'm ready to plead with him, to beg him to stay. I'm so frightened that I don't know what to do, and more afraid that I'll lose him.

Jonathan takes my hand and presses it to his lips. He continues to speak, but I can't hear his voice. Slowly, he rolls off me and pulls me from the spot under the bench in the corner of the room. In front of us is the security guard's wedding band and a trail of blood that leads back to his broken body on the other side of the room.

CHAPTER 15

JONATHAN

The art show isn't going the way I'd planned. Some lunatic bombed the damn thing. Cassie and I are lucky we're going to walk out in one piece, although we'll both have scars. A long gash mars the side of her perfect neck. There's so much blood when I look down that my terror turns into panic. A pool of crimson is under her head and seeping across the hard white floor.

"Cassie, it's all right. It's going to be all right." I stroke her face and whisper to her as I press her body to mine, waiting for the blasts to stop. My fucking ears aren't working and I can't tell if there are alarms going off yet, but we need medics. Now.

My eyes flick to the side and catch a flash of gold. There's a trail of blood that leads back to a fallen body. The old people who were on the other side of the room can't be seen. I feel completely useless and if I don't do something Cassie is going to bleed out on the floor.

When crap stops falling, I turn to see if it's over. Once I'm certain that I won't be shot, I whisper to Cassie, "I'm going for help. Don't move, Cass." As though she could. The truth is that I don't know what I'm saying. I can't even hear my own voice. Her eyes are glassy, wide with fear. Those beautiful lips move, begging for something that I can't hear. I rip off the bottom of my shirt and press it to her neck. Her eyes are glazing over and she shivers. I can't save her, I know I can't. My throat tightens as I realize what I have to do. Leaning in, I kiss her head. "I love you, Cass. Don't leave me. Hang on." It kills me to leave her, but I do.

Staggering to my feet, I look around at the museum. Canvases were blasted off the walls and there's debris everywhere. Chunks of concrete and wood line the floors. I'm walking like a fucking zombie, my feet won't move fast enough. I can't run. Shit, I can barely breathe. My ears don't work. It sounds like I'm walking through an empty cave, but there must be people screaming. There were people in here with us.

My phone. I dig into my pocket and pull it out as I stumble around. The screen is cracked and a few pieces of glass are missing. I flick it to life as I stagger toward what I think is the door. It's a bright opening that's flooded with light and white smoke. The screen comes to life and I dial. I don't know if they can hear me, but I scream into the phone and say where I am, and what's happened. I'm about to walk out into the sunlight flooding in from the next room when I see a piece of bent rebar. My foot stops just over the threshold. A gust of wind hits me in the face and I can see. I'm about to step through a hole in the wall and fall a couple of stories into the mob below. The phone tumbles out of my hand as my arms swing backward.

"Shit," I gasp, and press my back to the wall, trying to stop my sluggish momentum. My foot swings clumsily into the opening as my body lurches backward. I fall to the floor, instead of hitting the pavement below, and cough up a lung. There's tons of crap floating through the air. It flutters to the floor like gray pieces of snow.

I've crossed the room. This is the spot that was reserved for a painting that hadn't been installed yet. There was a temporary one in its place—not Gray's new piece. That means Cassie is across from me. As I try to make my way back to her, I see the old guy and his wife. He's hovering over her, holding her hand with tears flowing from his eyes. He says something to me as he tugs at his wife's lifeless arm. There's a thin cut on her forehead, but it shouldn't have killed her, and yet, she's not breathing. I can see it from where I stand. Her chest is still and her lips are turning an ungodly color.

Cassie is breathing, so I linger. Just for a second. I'm a selfish bastard, I know, but I can't lose Cassie. Not like this. I always thought if I never saw her again, it'd be because she got sick of my flirting and told me off. Things can't end like this.

I'm not really thinking at this point. My brain keeps running in circles, telling me to get the hell out, but I don't leave. More shit falls from the ceiling and shakes the ground. I can hear a distant thud, but it doesn't sound close. Not that I can tell.

Before I know what I'm doing, I'm at the old woman's side doing chest compressions. I stay like that until a medic pulls me away. They ask me stuff that I can't hear. I look behind me and say Cassie's name over and over again, but they don't answer me. A medic is pulling at my shirt, trying to remove it. I stop fighting. My body is covered in sweat and screaming at me to stop. The vise that's been squeezing my head tightens as sweat drips into my eyes. Hands are on me, and I fall to my knees and cough so violently that I expect to see my lung on the floor when I sit up.

When I glance across the room I can see police and paramedics. There are several people surrounding Cassie. "Is she all right?" They keep trying to help me, but I yell, and point at Cassie.

The medic next to me is a little thing with dark skin and slick black hair. Her hand lands lightly on my shoulder. Her mouth moves and she nods slowly, smiling at me weakly. Her lips say it's all right, and I finally stop fighting against everyone.

Today didn't turn out very well. Next time I take Cassie on a date, we'll have to roller skate across the spillway. It seems funny now. I finally found out why Cassie laughed at me when I tried to take a walk with her that day—Robyn said there are alligators in there and they walk across the road, happy to eat a few stupid pedestrians and go home.

Rationality is gone. I sit, breathing way too hard, and laugh, because if I don't laugh, I'm going to cry.

———

Cassie is next to me, a week later, and things have gotten interesting. They stitched up her neck and she's healing. We're not supposed to do much for a few days, just lay around is what the people at the hospital told us. So, we do. And that's how things begin to change. Cassie will take my hand and wrap my arm over her shoulder while I read her a book. She snuggles up next to me when we're watching TV and rests against my side. It's like she's actually mine, even though I know she'd never have me.

Sex hasn't come up, it rarely does, but tonight is going to break me. My willpower has dwindled to an all-time low, and I want her so badly that I can't think of anything else. When I close my eyes I picture Cassie in my arms and imagine sliding my hands along her silky skin, feeling every curve and muscle beneath my palm. I want to know every inch of her. I want to know what makes her writhe and what makes her knees weak. I want to hear that sigh of delight after she comes and hold her in my arms. I'm not a one woman guy, but I would be if I had a shot with her. But I don't. I'm not the guy she's looking for. To her, I'm used goods so she won't even consider me. Meanwhile, the scent of her hair, and her skin, is lodged in my mind and it's all I can do to breathe like a normal person while she lays next to me.

We're at my uncle's mansion, laying in the yard, and staring up at the sky. It's an inky black with a spattering of glittering stars. One of my arms is around Cassie's shoulders, and the other is at my side with my hand on my stomach. The scent of honeysuckle and Cassie's shampoo fills my head. I want to roll over and kiss her, but I don't. I just lay still and stare at the sky, wondering what kind of hell I've thrown myself into by allowing her to linger in this in-between place that's past friendship, but not lovers.

She touches the stiches on her neck absentmindedly. "I should be glad this wasn't worse, but it's going to leave a nasty scar."

"It won't, so you don't have to worry about it, but in the off chance that it does, well, no one in their right mind is going to be looking at your neck." She smiles and elbows me in the side lightly. "What are you jabbing me for with those pointy things? It's the truth. You're hot. Learn to live with it." Turning my face toward her, I stare at the smoothness of her cheek and fight the urge to touch, and trail my fingers over her soft flesh. I look away quickly and suck in the night air and let it out in a rush. I'm so drawn to her—so pulled to her—that the thoughts never stop.

So, when Cassie sits up and looks down at me, all I can do is stare. She's amazing. Her dark hair is draped over her bare arms, and a little slinky tank top clings to her body, accentuating the fullness of her chest and her tiny waist. My eyes drift over her as she moves and before I can ask what she's doing, Cassie's fingers find my waist and start tickling.

"My elbows are not pointy! They're angular." Her fingers wiggle as I try not to laugh, but she has me. My lips curve up at the corners and I start to laugh when she finds the right spot. I'm not a particularly ticklish guy, but there are a couple of places that'll make me laugh uncontrollably and Cassie has found one.

"Angular is an understatement, and weren't we talking about your boobs?" My elbows are pinned to my sides as I try to tickle her, but I can't stop cracking up long enough to find her ticklish spot. She has to have one, so my hands move up and down her sides trying to find it.

"You're always talking about boobs. Come on, Jon, be original." she laughs as my fingers hit the back of her knee. It's the most wonderful sound. Cassie tries to kick me away, but we're a tangle of arms and legs, both laughing and rolling over the lawn.

We're sitting side by side as I paw at her calf and twist her around. Cassie goes face first into the grass with a yelp. "Okay, how about this…" I tickle the back of her knee with a gentle sweep of my finger and she bucks around on the lawn like a docked fish. She's screaming and laughing so hard that I doubt she can hear me over the threats she's spewing, so I say it. "You are the most amazing person I've ever met, despite your strange views on sex, and rolling around with you in the grass with clothes on is more fun than rolling around naked with someone else."

Cassie manages to sit up, and then laughs as she chest bumps me—hard. The chick launches her breasts at me, slams into my chest, and sends me sailing back into the ground. It wouldn't have happened if I was expecting it, but who the hell chest bumps? Shock is plastered across my face and I'm caught somewhere between smiling, laughing, and surprise.

"Naked with someone else," she mocks, and rips out a clump of grass as she sits down hard, straddling me. "Eat dirt, Jon Ferro!" Cassie's smile is bigger than I've ever seen it. Her eyes are lit up and sparkling. For a brief moment, she's not holding back. I have all of her. This is as close to her heart as I'll ever get. I'm lost in thought, so my reaction time sucks. I barely manage to turn my face to the side as she tries to force-feed me grass.

"You chest bumped me?" Yeah, my brain is still in shock. I'm trying to piece together how she ended up on top of me. Her warm thighs cradle my hips as she squeezes tight, trying to stay there. She thinks I'm going to toss her off. Like that'll ever happen.

"You're two steps behind, Ferro." The clump of grass and dirt makes a pass for my mouth again. I manage to snatch Cassie's wrist and pull it down to the ground, so she falls flat against my chest. She gasps and then giggles, but I don't let go.

"Or two steps ahead. It depends on how you count."

She laughs and looks into my eyes. "And, what are you counting? How many times you can eat dirt?"

I shake my head, loving every second of this. "No, not at all."

"Then what—?" Her voice cuts off suddenly and the smug smile slips off her face. She catches my meaning and a full blush spreads across her cheeks. Even though it's dark, I know the look. The way she tries to hide her eyes and bury her face is fine by me. Cassie laughs and leans forward, pressing into my shoulder.

My heart pounds violently and I try to sit up and get her off of me, but Cassie laughs and looks down at me. "Oh, no, you're not going anywhere." She pins my shoulders to the ground with her hands.

Leaning over me she looks like heaven with those big dark eyes and full pink lips. Swallowing hard, I look up at her. Cassie's chest rises and falls too quickly, like she's nervous. Her grin flickers and fades until the only thing I see are those eyes. It feels like she's tied a line to my chest, and at this closeness it tightens, demanding that we close the space. I want her body pressed to mine so badly. I'm afraid she's going to realize what's happening and pull away, but she stays where she is.

Gazes locked, I loosen my grip on her wrists and slide my hands up her arms, feeling her soft skin. Cassie stiffens, but she doesn't tell me to stop, so I don't. My palms slip over her arms and shoulders before traveling down her back to her waist. For a moment it feels like I'm falling. The sensation of having her in my arms is unreal. But, when my hands reach her waist, it's over. I can't cup her ass or slide my hands anywhere else, so I linger there, feeling her ribs expand as she breathes. Those big eyes remain locked on mine and her pink lips part like she's going to speak, but Cassie remains silent.

I feel her thighs tense through her denim shorts as I start to feel my jeans tighten through the crotch. I can't hide how much I want her, and I know she has to feel it, but she doesn't comment on my aroused state. Instead, she takes hold of my wrists, and slips them under the hem of her shirt. I don't know what she's doing, and I'm too afraid to ask. I'm lost in the moment and right then, I'd do anything for her. So I place my hands against her hot, slick skin and rub my thumb against her back slowly, waiting for her to pull away.

Although it's night, the weather has been relentless. It's been close to a hundred degrees during the day and nights haven't cooled off much. The plan had been to go swimming tonight, but we never made it to the pool. Somehow we ended up stargazing, laying in each other's arms on the lawn.

My voice catches at the back of my throat, "Cassie…" I try to warn her how close I am to breaking, how much I want to throw her to the ground and make love to her.

"Please, Jon." Her voice is barely there, a whisper at most.

I don't know what she wants, because it can't be what I think she wants. This is a bad idea. I try to get up, but she's sitting on me. That perfect ass is so close to my hands. Hell, my hands are on her skin, under her shirt. That's the go-ahead to feel-up any other woman, but for some reason my hands are anchored to her waist. I'm paralyzed. I want to move, but I can't. Okay, I don't want to move, but I know I should, and for Cassie I would… But, the way she's looking at me combined with the weight of her body against mine is commandeering my thoughts. My fingers tense, and I try not to hold onto her even though her skin feels like heaven in my hands.

She sucks in a small breath, leans down and presses a kiss to my cheek. The moment her lips touch my skin I suck in air like there'll never be enough. Cassie lingers with her face next to mine, and her hand plays in my hair, curling it around her finger. She seems to be lost in thought. Several minutes pass before she says, "Sometimes things don't happen the way I thought they would. I want things, Jon, and I want them with you. I don't know what to do."

Stroking her hair, I answer, "I'm not *thee* guy, Cass. I wish to God I was, but—"

She doesn't let me finish. Her hand finds my face and she starts trailing the pad of her finger over my cheek and down to my mouth. She sits up slightly so she can see what she's doing. When Cassie's finger touches the corner of my mouth, my lips part, and a small gasp passes my lips. Her soft touch slips over my upper lip, tracing the bow so gently. It's taking a massive amount of willpower to stay still and let her do what she wants, and I wish to God that I could know what she's thinking, because it seems like she's changing her mind. Cassie's not talking and there's a pensive look on her face. It's not blind lust that I see.

Cassie's touch drifts to my lower lip, and as she slips it across my mouth she leans in and presses her lips just to the side of mine. I feel her heart pounding hard and fast as she lays on my chest again. Cassie cradles my face in her hands and I want to die because I can't have her. At the same time, I can't deny her this, even though it's making me crazy. I've never wanted someone so much in my entire life. My hands fist at my sides and I tear holes into the lawn, so that I won't touch her the way I want to. Everything within me wants to cup her face and kiss her back.

This is new for me, so I let my thoughts drift as my eyes close and I enjoy the way she touches me. Every time her hands sweep over me, the tension thickens.

I wonder if the bomb threw her the way it did me. Since the museum, I keep wondering if I've wasted my life. If everything ended there, what regrets would I have? Time after time the question surfaces in my mind, and I don't want to think about it because I can't change the one thing I regret most. I'll never have a shot with Cassie, no matter how much I change, because it's not the future that matters to her, it's the past and I can't change that.

So I keep my mouth shut and my eyes closed, and get lost in the moment. Things like this don't happen between us. Cassie is always so careful to keep her distance. Chance landed us in this position and I'm not ending it. I'd wrap my arms around her and hold on tight if I knew that it wouldn't spook her, because that's what frightens me most—that Cassie will realize what she's doing and stop. Or even worse, she'll regret it.

Cassie's hands sweep over me like she's memorizing the planes of my face. Her warm breath becomes shallower as her breathing quickens. The small kisses started off as a quick peck, but now her lips linger and they inch closer and closer to my mouth. Then something changes. I'm not sure who started it, but her hips are moving slowly, rubbing against mine as her thighs tighten around me. It breaks me. I can't keep my hands off of her.

I take her waist in my hands and pull her down against me, trying to still her. I'm already hard, and the way she's gyrating against me is going to make me lose it. I don't know what I expect, but when she looks down at me, every rational thought flies out of my brain. Those eyes—the way they look at me in this moment – say everything.

My pulse surges when I realize what I see in her eyes. Cassie changed her mind.

Cassie's voice is softer this time, more timid. She reaches for my hands, and puts them back under the hem of her shirt and draws them higher. My fingers slip over her skin as I fight every urge building inside of me. Cassie sucks in a sharp breath, as she guides my hands to her bra. I feel the sheer fabric and her warm skin beneath. Her nipples are taut, pushing against the material, demanding to be freed. Her eyes are locked with mine while she does it. "Touch me, Jon. Please."

I don't pull my hands away when she drops my wrists. Cassie watches me for a moment, but when I smooth my thumb over her nipple her back goes straight and her thighs tighten against mine. Her head tips back and she holds her breath until I do it again. I'm drowning in lust, unable to think. My hands are filled with her breasts and I'm more turned on than I've ever been, because it's her. I tease, working her nipple through the thin fabric, pinching and pulling gently, which makes her gasp again and again. Her back arches and it begins again—Cassie's hips start to sway. They move slowly at first, probably because of what I'm doing to her breasts, and the more she moves, the more I touch her. The heat between us is scorching. I want to bury my dick inside of her and push in deeper and harder until she comes and screams my name.

Fuck, I can't think. We need to stop. She's going to regret this. I can't let her do it. The thought is lost as Cassie's slow grinding goes wild. She rides me, rubbing against me like she can't stop. Her tits bounce in my hands as she slams into me. Little sounds come from the back of her throat. She tries to hide them at first and then gives up. I know I should stop her, but I can't. I can't do anything except this.

Breathless, Cassie raises her hands and rests her arms on top of her head. She rocks her hips over and over against me, with only a few layers of clothing between us. Her pace becomes frantic and she suddenly throws herself down onto my chest. Her nails bite through my shirt and into my shoulders as I grab her ass and pull her down harder. I moan incoherently as she rides me. Each thrust is harder and faster and I don't want her to stop. I want to see her face when she comes.

Reality slams into me. She can't come. Not like this. Not with me. She'll never forgive herself. My body is so fucking hot and I need her so much, but I don't want her to hate me in the morning. I force myself to wrap my arms around her and crush her against my chest so that she can't move.

Cassie gasps. She's laying on top of me and I can feel her heart racing inside her chest. I manage to say, "We need to stop." At first she struggles, but after a moment she stops. Her body loses some of the tension and she trembles. "You'll regret this, baby. I know you will." My hand strokes her back as we lay there together. I wonder if it was stupid to stop her. Maybe she changed her mind a while ago and never said anything, but I can't chance her hating me. I couldn't bear that.

I hold her tight, not wanting to let go, when she rolls off of me. She speaks into my shoulder, avoiding my eyes. "I'm sorry, I didn't mean to—"

Reaching for her, I play with the long curls hanging down her back. "You don't have to apologize. You can use my body whenever you want. I could have made you come, and fuck, I wanted that more than anything, but I lov—" I catch myself just as the word is about to leave my lips. A cold sensation trickles through my heart when I realize what I was going to say. *I love you, Cass. I couldn't do that to you.* I love her. The seeds of fear scatter and make me shiver.

Cassie glances down at me, her face unreadable, before she lowers herself and lays at my side. She buries her face in my chest as I hold onto her. "But what?"

I consider saying it, but I can't. The words are lodged somewhere in the back of my throat. I hedge, "What made you do that?"

She shrugs. "I shouldn't have."

"Did you change your mind, Cass?"

"Maybe." She presses her lips together and is quiet for a few minutes. "I don't know what I think about things anymore. I was so sure before I met you, but now—I just don't know. You probably think I'm silly giving this much thought to being with one guy. Meanwhile, you've been banging a different girl every night of the week since summer started." She rolls onto her side and looks up at me. For a second I think she's joking, but the soft smile on her face says otherwise. She doesn't realize what she's done to me.

Our eyes lock and the urge to pour my heart out overtakes me. I could laugh and agree with her, but I don't want to. I want my shot with Cassie Hale and this is it.

Lifting my hand to her face, I trail it over her soft skin and say, "You might think that, but the truth is, I haven't slept with anyone since I got here."

She blinks at me. "Why not?"

"Because I want you."

CHAPTER 16

CASSIE

There's no way he said it, but he did. I heard him. "You haven't had sex since you met me?" He shakes his head. His blue eyes are so dark, and they fixate on me unashamed. My body tenses and the feeling that I'm in over my head crashes into me again. It was a stupid idea to lay down with him. When I asked him to touch me, I meant for him to run his hands over my skin, but then I couldn't stop. I like the idea of Jon's hands on me, and I wanted to be in his arms—no, I wanted to lose myself in his arms. I wanted to feel that release as I came, and... Oh God.

As soon as the thought drifts through my mind, I bolt upright and sit on the grass next to him, clutching my knees like a lawn gnome. I'm so conflicted. Part of me wants to give in, but I've had this belief for so long. Abandoning it now seems foolish.

Am I a fool? Is my body so driven by lust that I can't control myself or is it more than that?

A very rational voice echoes in the back of my mind, *It's more than that, much more.*

"Cassie," Jon's hand is on my back as he sits up. It sends a shiver through me and it's impossible to deny how much I want him. How did this happen? I'm ready to jump up and run all the way back to Aunt Paula's house, but Jon takes my wrist. I glance at him out of the corner of my eye, watching him as he lifts my hand close to his face. "Tell me what you want, baby. I'll give it to you. All you have to do is ask me."

A jagged breathe escapes me and I glance over at him. "I don't know what I want. I want more, but I don't want to throw away everything I believe so fast. I don't want to regret this, Jon."

"So let's do a little more, something you won't regret. Something that's fairly innocent, but feels like more." He's watching me, waiting for my approval, but I don't know what he means. The question must be written on my face because Jon smiles softly and takes my hand.

Glancing at him out of the corner of my eye, I watch as he lifts my wrist to his lips. Jon turns it over so the soft part, just below my palm, is nearly on his mouth. When he breathes, something stirs inside of me. I imagine his mouth on my wrist and am surprised how hard it makes my heart pound. A jolt of tingles shoots through me when I think about it, and it's strange because I've never thought about it before. I avert my eyes quickly, but he doesn't drop my hand.

"What if I kissed you here?" His finger presses to the inside of my wrist, making my stomach flutter. He draws a circle before I feel his eyes on my cheek again. Jon leans toward me, trying to catch my eye. "It's a pulse point, one of the most sensitive spots on your body. It'll make you feel good without changing everything you believe tonight. Right? I mean, you didn't have wedding night plans that involved wrist kissing, did you?" He smiles at me and leans in close, touching his forehead to mine.

"No, I didn't really think about it before now." I feel silly asking, but I ask anyway, "Have you done this before? Of course you have. Why'd I even say that? You've been—" I begin to prattle as my face turns red and I look away.

Jon hooks his finger under my chin and forces our gazes to meet. The corners of his mouth turn up, "I haven't done this before. It's too sweet and innocent, so I blew right past it. But I thought you'd like it. This kind of kiss is a middle ground. It's not as intimate as some kisses, but more so than others."

Nervous energy flutters through my stomach, as I lay back on the grass, and lift my hand to him. It's nonverbal permission. We're alone, in the dark, far from the house and the noise. I close my eyes and feel my heart race in my chest as Jon lays next to me and takes my hand. My stomach flips when I feel his breath on my skin and my skin becomes hypersensitive. When his lips brush against my wrist, a surprised sound comes from the back of my throat and I tense up next to him.

When he pauses between kisses, he says, "Tell me if you change your mind."

I can barely breathe. "I will."

He presses his mouth against my inner wrist again and I gasp louder this time. The sensation scares me, making me feel completely vulnerable as tingles shoot through every inch of my body. I resist it and try to fight back the surge of emotions that threaten to overtake me. I stare at him as his tongue sweeps across my skin.

He sees me and smiles. "I bet you have a toe fetish."

"I do nahhhh…" My offense had a lot more to it before he kissed me again. His lips move over that one spot, licking, sucking, and tasting me. My eyes close and I try to savor the sensations, but I can't. They're so strong, and every time his mouth touches me, I want to wrap my legs around him.

The kisses grow hotter, and longer, making me want to writhe slowly on the grass, but I fight it and hold my hips still. I'm afraid of what will happen if I let go and enjoy the sensations. I don't know what it'll do or what it means. Jon's my friend, but his lips are attached to my wrist and the urges he's evoking aren't friendly. I want his hands tangled in my hair with his naked body pressed to mine. I want to know the taste of his kiss and learn the curve of his mouth. I'm not asexual, I've had these thoughts before, but not like this. These are clear desires, dreams almost. They're things I hope for, wishes that I'm too afraid to recognize.

Jon's eyes are closed and I watch his face as he kisses me. That turns out to be a mistake, because his expression is so carnal, so sexual that the pulsing between my legs is unbearable. Closing my eyes, I take my free hand and claw the ground next to me, arching my back as I do it. I want to surrender to the feelings. I want them to overtake me and pull me under, but I can't. I cling to my mind even though it's trying to abandon me. I can't think. I just want his mouth—his hot, wet tongue—to lick my stomach and slide up higher and higher, inch by inch, to my aching breasts. Every kiss of my wrist pushes me closer to the edge until I'm clinging there with everything I have.

Breathless, Jon stops and looks over at me. "Let go, Cassie. I won't hurt you, baby. Let go."

I clutch the ground and rip out the grass. My chest rises and falls too quickly. It feels like my heart will rupture inside my body and I'll die if I let go, if I surrender my control. Jon smiles softly and sits next to me. He shifts me so that my head is in his lap, and I'm lying on my back, looking up at the sky. His thighs are around my shoulders, cradling me, as Jon lifts my other wrist to his lips.

My body tenses as I fight the sensation of wicked urges. I can't give into him, but I want to. I want to let myself feel whatever it is to be lost in Jonathan Ferro. My eyes flicker as I gasp, caught in the middle. It's like I'm desperately clutching a ledge, about to fall off. My fingers are tearing and my nails are ripping, but I can't let go.

That's when I tense and lift off his lap slightly. Jon's other hand guides me back down and strokes my cheeks. "Trust me, Cass. Let go."

Those words, they push me over the edge and my body relaxes in his lap. Jon strokes my skin as his lips travel over my skin. Tingles shoot through me like fireworks, arching my back, and pushing my pulse faster. I tug my arm away, but Jon locks it to his lips, continuing to press his mouth and sweeping his tongue over my sensitive flesh. My jaw falls open and I moan as my chest lifts again, needing the touch of his hand on my breast. I'm an animal in this state. I can't think and I don't want to. I want to feel, and I do. I feel more and want more. His mouth is heaven and I'm aching for him to touch me.

This isn't sex. I have no idea what this is, but it's not what I imagined I'd be doing with my husband on my wedding night—or ever. It's so different, and I want it so much. Moaning his name, I turn my face toward his. "Jon."

My body is tightening into thick coils. I feel them inside of me as I grow hotter and the place between my legs throbs for his attention. Gasping, I tilt my head back and close my eyes. My heart races so hard that I think I'm going to die.

At that moment, Jon whispers in my ear, "I love you, Cass."

Those words. They jerk me out of my stupor and I dart out of his lap. I can't catch my breath and don't trust my knees to hold, but I jump up anyway. With my hand to my heart, I stare at him.

Jon's on his feet and stepping toward me. "Cass…" He lifts his hands to me, but I'm paralyzed.

Fear and mistrust mingle inside my mind as panic races through me. I try to stop it, but I can't. He doesn't love me. Guys like him say things like that to girls like me because it's what we want to hear, not because it's true. I'm suddenly livid, caught between tears and anger.

"Do you say that to all the girls? Or is it just for the ones who are stupid like me?" I don't mean any of it, but the words pour out of my mouth, and I can't stop them.

Jon steps toward me with a wounded look on his face. "You don't mean that."

"How am I supposed to believe you? Tell me, Jon! I need to know—" I'm sob-yelling now, gasping for air that won't come.

He steps toward me again. "You know me, Cass. Better than anyone. I'm not lying to you. I couldn't make up the anguish I feel when you're not there."

"Stop!" I hold my hands to my ears like it'll keep me from hearing him, but it doesn't. His voice rings through.

"Stop, what? Stop loving you? Because I tried that, Cass, and it didn't work. I've completely and totally fallen for you. There's no way out."

And then his arms slip around my waist and he pulls me against his chest. The tears start and won't stop, but I have no idea why. He said exactly what I wanted to hear. All I have to do is believe him.

"Do you love me, Cassie?" His voice is uncharacteristically vulnerable and catches on my name. Jon tilts his head as he lifts my chin. Our gazes lock and I've never been more frightened of anything in my entire life. Even when the museum was falling to pieces around me, things seemed more solid—more certain.

But I know how I feel. I just have to find the words. I smile through my tears, and nod. "I love you, Jonathan Ferro."

CHAPTER 17

JONATHAN

In a matter of moments, my entire world changed. She loves me. She said so. By the time I drop her off at her aunt's house and prance through Uncle Luke's front door, it's nearly 3:00am. Time means nothing to me right then. I feel invincible. There's a huge smile on my face and I have to seriously control my urge to dance through the house and sing. She loves me! I've never been in love before. I wonder how long I'll feel like this, and how long the smile will remain tattooed to my lips.

As I take the steps two at a time, I hear Uncle Luke's voice. "Jonny, we need to talk."

I freeze half way up the staircase and look down at him. He's still dressed, wearing everything except his favorite boat shoes. The look on his face says something's wrong—very wrong.

I'm frozen. If I go down to him my high will crash and break into a million pieces, and I'm greedy. I don't want to let it go just yet. "What's wrong?" I'm still facing the wrong way, with both hands plastered to the railing, like I'm going to head to my room.

"Jonny, I don't know how to say this and I'd prefer that you didn't topple down the stairs when you hear. Please come here."

That turns me around, but my feet don't want to move. My mind races through possible scenarios that would make him say something like that, but short of someone dying, I can't think of anything else. I force my feet to the kitchen and stand at the threshold, as if not actually entering the room will protect me from whatever is about to happen.

Uncle Luke pinches the bridge of his nose and glances up at me. "I wish I had better news, kid. I really do." He holds out a hand for me to take a seat, but I don't move. I stare at him with my lips pressed together, waiting for him to drop the bomb. I'm braced and ready for it.

"Just tell me."

He sniffs and looks away as he rubs his tired eyes with the heel of his hands. Luke reaches for a paper that's on the counter and tosses it to me. "A friend dropped this off. He thought I'd want to know. When I saw it…" He shakes his head, not finishing the sentence.

Ice shoots through my veins as I flip the paper to the front page. I don't want to look at it, but I have to. My stomach twists in knots as I look down. Boldfaced letters stare back at me, robbing me of breath. It feels like I've been sucker punched so hard that my knees give out. The paper falls to the floor as I stagger, grabbing the counter to hold me upright. "No, Uncle Luke. This isn't real. It can't be."

Luke races toward me, grabbing my arm. "I'm afraid it is. No amount of money will make this go away. The papers are already headed out. Come morning, everyone will see this, Jonathan—including your mother."

"No. There's no way. She wouldn't." I shake him off and pace the room, trying to piece it together, but the pieces only fit into one shape. "Tell me it's not real! Tell me she didn't do this to me!"

"I'm sorry, Jonathan." It's the only thing he says about her, about Cassie. "The first flight I could get you on is in the afternoon. We should put off the media for at least a little while, but your mother is another story."

"I cost you a hell of a present for babysitting me." I say it into the air, as I stare out the window. How could I be so wrong?

"That doesn't matter, Jonny. It's just stuff." I glance at him and wonder why he doesn't want to kill me. "There are other things that take priority. Head up to your room and stay there until we leave for the airport."

I do as he says without a fight because I don't have it in me. The hours tick by so slowly that they feel like weeks. By the time the sun rises, I've been sitting by the window in my room for hours. I see her smiling face race up the walk to the front entry. Cassie presses the bell and Luke opens the door. He threatens to fill her ass with buckshot if she doesn't leave, but she won't.

It kills me, but I manage to get up and walk halfway down the stairs so she can see me. Cassie stops talking and gives me the most pitiful look. "Jon, I—"

"I don't want to hear it." That's all I say. At least I think that's all I said. Seeing her there is like letting someone reach into my chest and rip out my heart. I can't stand it, so I turn and walk away. Maybe I'm in shock, or maybe she broke my heart. Either way, I'm fucked. When I get home all Hell is going to break free and it's because of her. Eventually anger will fill the memories of her, but in the meantime they sting like a mother.

Cassie Hale held my heart in the palm of her hand, and crushed it.

CHAPTER 18

~THE PRESENT~

CASSIE

When I hear Jonathan's voice a lifetime of memories flood my mind, but the one that sticks out is from the art show and the way the air was drenched with sulfur and charred wood—and the way Jonathan pressed me to the ground, using his body to shield me. He barely knew me then, but he did it without a second thought. Sometimes when I close my eyes at night, I wonder how differently my life would have been if I didn't have my stupid, naïve, morals back then, if I kissed him and he kissed me back—if I let him make love to me. But there's no time to think about that now.

I have seconds to sneak out of the room, but Beth is on my arm, hissing in my ear. "Oh no you don't. You fought for this job and now you're keeping it." Beth laces her fingers together and jerks me close. We're hip to hip as my heart slams into my rib cage.

"Beth, I have to go." I try to peel her fingers off my arm, but she doesn't release me, so I do the only thing I can think of and drag her skinny ass across the floor, toward the door.

She shrieks, "Oh my God! Stop!" When I ignore her, she drops to her knees while hanging on my arm. Wrapping her arms around my waist, she clings to me like a slutty koala bear covered in glitter. "Cassie, think this through!"

I make an undignified sound as she slows me down. I'm going to lose my balance and fall on my ass if I don't pry her off. Attempting to twist out of her grip isn't working. "Damn it, Beth! Let go!"

"No! This is the biggest mistake of your life! It'll put you right back where you don't want to be, and once you walk away you can't come back." Gripping my corseted waist tighter, she shifts her weight and throws me off balance, but I recover and continue to wrangle her to the door. "Hercu-freak!"

"Beth, I swear to God, I'm going to kill you if you don't let me go right now." She won't let go—Beth's good like that. When she thinks I'm making a colossal misstep, she'll dig in her heels and do everything she can to prevent it, but seeing Jonathan Ferro would be a mistake, especially after everything that happened. I'm wearing next to nothing and am covered in glitter. The baby oil on our skin is making it really difficult for Beth to keep a hold on me. Her hands slip down to my hips and her fingers dig in.

We're both whisper-screaming at each other and by the time her arms slip down to my thighs, I can barely move. That's when her death grip suddenly slips, and she falls to the floor without releasing me. Her arms act as a lasso around my legs. They slip to my knees, and then to my ankles, before I come tumbling down. Beth makes an *oof* sound as she lands on her boobs and snatches my ankles as I try to crawl away.

It's at that ungodly moment that we're spotted. I'm actually crawling across the floor on my hands and knees with Beth slithering behind me with her fingers wrapped around my foot. There's a wake of sparkles on the floor behind us.

"Peter has no idea what he's missing." His voice is a whisper, but it catches my ear just as Beth's arms yank me back and my face hits the floor.

"I doubt that," Sean Ferro's voice makes us freeze. It booms through the room with a clear undertone that demands we stop.

Body tense, I release Beth at the same time she lets go of me. I don't lift my face, I don't look Jonathan in the eye. Between heartbeats, I hope he's forgotten me, or at the very least, no longer wants to kill me because of what I did to him in Mississippi. I'm close to trembling as I try to remain completely still, but my muscles disobey me and twitch. I grab my wrist tightly and try to hide every emotion that is swelling within me, ready to burst across my face at any moment.

"Come on, Sean. Pete's a man. Every guy loves to see shit like that. Am I right ladies?" Jonathan is walking towards us. I don't lift my face, but Beth does.

She speaks and tries to take the attention off of me. "Most men do, sir."

Jonathan is standing adjacent to me with his hands in his pockets. It's the same thing he did when we were younger. It hides his uncertainty from his brother. "See? Sean, let's just keep these two. I already told their manager to forget about the wait staff. As cool as it would have been to see the waitresses rip off their shirts during dinner, that part's cancelled. And it's a goddamn bachelor party. We can keep these two here and if Pete wants to come in, he can. If not, he'll hang out in the main hall. No harm, right?"

Sean stands there perfectly rigid. His eyes sweep over Beth and me. There's too much silence and I swear that he can hear my pulse pounding. It's so damn loud that everyone should be able to hear it. Sean steps toward me, like he senses my fear. "Why were you two fighting?"

Beth laughs. "We weren't fighting for real. It's staged." She moves toward Sean and tries to take his arm, but he evades her and steps closer to me.

"Is that so?"

"Yeah, it's part of the show," Beth lies. I see her feet behind Sean's. He's right in front of me, towering over my small form, staring holes in the top of my head. I won't look up.

"Very well, I want to hear it from her."

Beth laughs nervously. "Uh, she can't talk, Mr. Ferro."

"Really?"

"Yeah, horrible boating accident when she was a kid. She looks down like that to cover a nasty scar on her throat. You can kind of see it under the make up on the side of her neck. Don't tell our boss. We're not supposed to have scars."

Fuck! Why did she say that? I continue to stare at my toes, but now I have two sets of eyes on me instead of one. Jonathan stands off to the side where the scar is located and I hope to God he doesn't make me look at him. I'm not certain if he recognizes me or not.

Jonathan is watching me closer now, his eyes sweep over the side of my face again and again as if he knows he's missing something. For a moment, there's no smile on his lips, no laughter in his voice. When he finally steps away, he shakes his head and says, "Maybe you're right, Sean. This is too much for Pete. We should send them all home. Will you walk this lovely woman out?"

In that second, things change. I glance at Beth out of the corner of my eye. She starts to sputter excuses as to why she can't leave me, but Jonathan cuts her off, "It's all right. I've made arrangements so you two will still be paid. Sean, go pay their manager."

Sean sighs like he's irritated and turns on his heel after watching me a moment too long. Beth starts to speak, but Jonathan talks over her. "Please, follow Sean out." Although Jonathan's tone is softer than Sean's, Beth still does as he asks which makes me want to kill her.

After a moment the room fills with silence. The silvery curtains flutter behind Jonathan as we stand in front of one another, both of us staring at our feet. When he glances up and tries to meet my gaze, I don't let him. I keep my chin buried in my chest and stand there perfectly rigid with my mind melting inside my head. *I can't... I can't...* keeps replaying over and over again, like a scratched CD.

Jonathan swallows hard. "So, you're a mute now?"

My lips quiver as they part. No words come out, but my heart tries to. I snap my mouth shut and go to turn away, but he catches my arm—which is a strict no-no with this job. The action makes me look up at him, and as soon as I do it I realize my mistake. I couldn't resist his eyes the first time, but now—it's worse.

We didn't part on the best of terms the last time I saw him, actually he thought I used him. Me. Like that would ever happen. The thing is, I didn't fight to correct his misconception. There were reasons, the main one was that I thought he'd see the truth anyway, but he didn't.

The Ferro men all have that hot temper, but it's Jonathan who'll hold a grudge until he's older than dirt. Jonathan's eyes sweep over my face, trail down my neck to my corset and lift again. "I knew you had a peculiar view on sex, but stripping is usually further down the road than kissing." Damn, he sounds bitter, and the way he spits out the words like they're pitch forks doesn't help any. That smug, arrogant, smirk on his face tells me everything I need to know. He hates me. Fine, it's better that way. I have no desire to rehash the shit I've lived through—the things he doesn't know about.

I reach for a good comeback and come up empty handed. I settle for a timeless classic, "Go to hell," I growl and try to yank my arm away, but he holds on tight.

"I'm already there, sweetheart, and honestly quite shocked to find you here." His eyes burn into me like twin flames of pure heat. The intensity sends a jolt through my core that explodes in my stomach. His touch is making my brain short out, so I twist my wrist free and glare at him. His eyes dip to the floor and his tone changes— back to light and fluffy—like nothing could possibly be wrong, like his brother isn't going to kill him when I'm through with him. "So," he beams his pearly whites at me, "how's your evening going, Cassie?"

I manage to force my lips into a smile. This game of his used to drive me nuts. Do you have any idea how long it took me to unearth the real Jonathan Ferro only to lose him because of that stupid—forget it. I know how to play the fucking game, too. I've mastered the craft of false flirting and sincere smiles that are as fake as Gretchen's boobs. I can handle this. I can outmaneuver Jonathan Ferro and be back at the club within the hour.

My voice is sultry when I speak, utterly controlled. "Perfect. Never better. You know, I wasn't going to say anything, but that little spat with your brother back there was kind of cute. I like how fast he derailed you. It was so noble of you to bend over and take one for the team." My chest feels so tight that my ribs ache, and I can't breathe, but I don't let the confident grin slip from my lips. This is a game with him, and I know he wants to get the best of me, but he won't. Not this time. Those words were lashes and they strategically struck him blow by blow until that fancy boy smile fell off his face.

I shoulder past him, intending to leave, when he laughs. The sound is light and carefree, like he thinks I'm humorous. I glance back at him to see his head tip to the side and his hands slip out of his pockets. That nervous, twitchy, finger thing he did back when I first met him is gone. There's no telling that he isn't pleased, with the exception of my heart racing like I'm about to be slaughtered.

"Actually, you'll be the one bending over and taking one for the team. You see, I didn't give Sean exactly what he wanted—this is a Ferro party and I have a reputation to uphold—so I made arrangements with your manager to keep the sluttiest girl he brought. Imagine my surprise when it turned out to be you."

My hand flies, but before it strikes his cheek Jonathan catches my wrist. He holds it tight and tosses it aside like I'm trash. "You were always a cheap date, huh, Cassie?"

"Fuck you."

"Later, baby." He grins at me as he turns on his heel and heads toward the door.

"You'll never have me."

A grin dances across his face and he turns around to walk out backward. His fingers lift and point at me like twin pointers. "I'm not the one wearing just glitter, 'cause yeah, that top doesn't count. You pretty much fell out of it when you were rolling around on the floor with your friend before." He winks at me as he exits the door, "The stage is all yours, Cassie Hale. Knock yourself out."

CHAPTER 19

JONATHAN

Fuck. This can't be happening. How is it that things always go to shit when I need them to work out? Cassie Hale. Damn it. I slam my fist into the bathroom wall and swear. The old guy seated with the towels in the corner acts like I don't exist. I lean into the wall, curling my arm, and rest my head there for a second. It's fucking pounding.

Cassie. The last time I saw her, she screwed me over. I spilled my guts to her one summer when we were kids, and she told me all this shit and I believed it. Obviously, I got played worse than I thought. She's a goddamn stripper. The thought makes me sick. Even though I know she stabbed me in the back, I can't stand the thought of the other guys seeing her naked. It feels like someone reached into my chest, grabbed hold of my heart, and ripped the fucker out. I can't breathe.

Why is she here? It's been years since I've seen her, years since she pulled her shit, so why is she sliding around on the floor? And why now? Fate's a bitch, a goddamn bitch.

Pushing off the wall, I walk over to the sink and wash my face off. I need to pull it together. She can't see that she has any effect on me at all. I take a towel from the guy and hand him a fifty, and say, "You didn't see anything."

"Of course." He smiles at me and pockets the cash.

When I hit the hallway, Trystan falls in step beside me. "So, Peter and the strippers…"

"There's only one left and he can take care of her."

Trystan looks at me weirdly, but doesn't say anything. He doesn't know about Cassie or any of that shit. All that stuff happened before I met him. I glance over. "Sean wants to rip your heart out."

Trystan laughs, "Sean needs to relax."

"Like that'll ever happen." I shove my hands into my pockets and push into the main room, looking for Peter.

"We need to get Pete to the private party room." A plan forms in my mind. I want to humiliate her and crush her like she crushed me. Maybe doing it this way is a dick move, but I'm an asshole, so it's okay. The truth is, I can't fathom why she stabbed me in the back. I thought she cared about me, but as soon as she had the chance, Cassie bit me on the ass like a rabid dog.

I grab a few more guys as I track down Pete. Bryan Ferro is a cousin, and a couple of years older than me, and he falls in step with Trystan. The two of them will get me in more trouble than I'm already in, but what the hell. I mean, you only live once, right? Bryan is the kind of guy that can make anything sound like a great idea. The man has a golden tongue. He's a snake charmer. Any bitch will fall on her knees just to hear him talk. And Trystan is frequently followed around by a slew of topless women. Who wouldn't like that? Our group collects more guys as we walk through. The Trystan, Bryan, Jon trifecta is too much to pass up. Everyone knows, if you want to be where it's at to hang around with us.

Everyone except Sean. Where the hell did he go? I glance around, but there's no sign of him. Sometimes I wonder if he has ovaries, he's so damn moody. But then again, I'd probably be moody too if I got dumped by a hooker. Peter told me this crazy ass story and I'm seriously wondering what the hell Sean was doing. The guy is brilliant, and utterly insane. When he gets an idea in his head, there's no way to smack it out. Sean's taken too many shots to the heart. He's a walking corpse like the rest of us, well, except for my other brother— Peter—who's sitting in the middle of a group of guys, smiling like he's king of the world. Dumb fucker, has no idea what he's in for.

After living with my parents, I don't know how anyone could think marriage is a good idea, but Peter's over there smiling like a fool.

"Jaded much?" Trystan says so only I can hear. I smile at him and shake my head, like he's crazy. "Just pointing out the obvious. The scowl on your face says too much man. Keep your thoughts to yourself, especially if you like this brother." He smacks his shoulder against mine and nods once. It's a warning, telling me to pull my shit together.

Wiping the bitter look off my face, I throw myself into the crowd. "Peter! My favorite brother!"

Pete smiles and hands me a beer. "Jonny! You weren't supposed to throw me a party. Sidney will kill me if she thinks I had a bachelor party."

"Do you see anything in here? No titties, no poles, no lap dances. It's utterly boring." I grab his phone and take a pic of the room. It looks like an ad for an old time bar, the kind where women weren't welcome. I shoot it over to his fiancée. "And you picked Sean to be your best man."

Peter laughs and has no idea what he's in for. "Sean can be a bitch when he doesn't get his way." All the guys around us laugh. We do a few rounds of shots, and I make sure Peter is off guard when I make the transition. "You're the best brother a guy could hope for, which is why there's no way in hell I'm giving you a boring-ass party like this."

"Jonny?" He gives me a look that says he'll tear me a new one later, but not now.

That's all the permission I need. I love Sidney, I really do, but she has to understand that this isn't personal. Grabbing his arm, I stand on one side and Bryan stands on the other. We flank him and pull him toward the door, saying, "Peter, I love you, man, but you're not marching into marriage without doing one last crazy thing, and that's why we're heading to the private party room."

Peter protests, but he won't make me feel bad. I'm an asshole. I shouldn't do this to him, but I have to crush Cassie for what she did to me. I can't let it go. She's trapped, and I intend to make her suffer.

CHAPTER 20

CASSIE

Fury rips through me like a whirlwind. My hands are clenched into fists as I watch him walk away. Briefly, I think about hurling a heel at the back of his head, but with my luck I'd kill him. I wander over to the stage and sit down hard on the edge. FML. Seriously. It can't get worse than this. Seeing Jonathan this way is humiliating enough, but add in the venom and it's nearly unbearable. I hold my face in my hands and lean forward, sucking in a deep breath before straightening up. I have to push him out of my head or I'm screwed.

This isn't the kind of job that I wanted, but I worked my ass off to get it and I'm not letting some Ferro twit throw me off my game so that I get tossed with the morning trash. I'm not trash. I don't let anyone treat me like I am, but Jonathan just blasted me to bits. My fingers drift to the scar on my neck. I remember everything, even though I said I didn't. I saw his frantic face and worried eyes. A piece of shrapnel sliced the side of my neck that day. Even though Jonathan tried to protect me, he couldn't do enough. He never thought he was good enough, and my moralistic high ground didn't help. If I knew then what I know now, I would have done things differently.

At least that's what I tell myself when I'm upset, like now. How am I supposed to strip in front of him? Damn it. I push myself up and have a heart attack when I bump into Sean Ferro. A startled yelp bursts from my mouth before I stumble backwards. He reaches out and steadies me, asking, "Who are you?"

It's not the question I expected. "I'm sorry, I didn't see you there."

"I'm well aware of that, and, since you're obviously not vocally compromised, I expect you to answer my question."

Oh God, another Ferro asshole that thinks he's entitled. The urge to roll my eyes and walk away is huge, but something about this guy makes the hairs on the back of my neck stand on end. He's a little bit scary, in a serial killer kind of way. I bet he could dump my body in the Connetquot River and be back before they finish dinner.

There's a smear of sparkles on his lapel. It looks like a giant lightening bug tried to make out with him. He snaps his fingers in front of my nose like I'm a dog. "Are you mentally impaired? I asked you a question."

"I don't have to tell you jackshit." I turn away, but I feel his eyes on my back. It creeps me out. The guy is a bundle of nerves. He stares at me like he wants to snap me in half.

Sean takes a step toward me and I hear his shoe scuff the floor. My heart hammers harder, smacking into my ribs. I've heard enough about Sean Ferro straight from Jonathan—enough to know that screwing with him is a death wish. The guy got shortchanged when God was handing out patience. He's always angry, the beauty in his features hidden by the hard lines of his mouth and judgmental eyes. Seriously, like he's one to pass judgment on anyone.

"I think you do." His voice makes my skin prickle. It's the axe murderer reaction.

Spinning on my heel, I round on him with my eyes pressed into thin slits. "And that's where you're wrong. Just because you're a Ferro doesn't mean you can do whatever you goddamn want." Trying to swallow the lump in my throat, I stare at him. Cobalt blue eyes stare back. Although I expect my answer to evoke anger, the corners of his mouth twitch, as if he's amused that I have enough of a spine to talk to him. Arrogant prick. Guys like him think they own girls like me. Just because I strip doesn't mean I'm devoid of conviction. People fail to realize that. Sometimes people have more choices. Sometimes people are handed a fucking fortune while others fall face first into the dust, completely alone.

So when some rich asshole starts with me, I don't back down. "Take your silver spoon and shove it up your ass." My voice is dripping with disdain. After the words fly, I expect Sean to be irate—I expect him to fly off the handle—maybe even try to force the answer he wants out of me, but the guy only laughs.

He fucking laughs in my face. "Wow. Just wow."

I glare at him. His reaction caught me off guard. No one likes to be insulted, but this guy acts like he loves it. What a freak. "Fuck off."

"You had me at, *you're wrong.*" He tilts his head back and looks me over as his arms fold over his chest. The designer suit he's wearing accentuates his frame, and I have no doubt that there's toned muscle under all that fabric. "Listen, Jonathan has enough issues and I can see that some things—"

"Jonathan? That's what you've gone nuts about?" I drop my gaze and the tension in my shoulders drops to the pit of my stomach like a lead ball. "You don't have to worry about Jonathan. He hates me. End of story."

"No, because he knows you. Beginning of story. Why does he know you? Obviously, he had no idea you'd be here tonight, which begs the question—who are you and how long have you known him?"

A vacant expression is on my face. I feel it inch across, and there's nothing I can do to stop it. Hearing Sean say those words pulls the emotions back from the void, from that hollow spot deep inside my chest where regret still lingers. There was no way to fix what happened, and the worst part was I didn't mean for it to occur. Yet, it was my fault. All of it. The look in Jon's eyes, it was so much like Sean's gaze now—a sincere plea for an answer.

"I'm no one to be concerned about, Mr. Ferro. After tonight, you'll never see me again and neither will Jon." Before Sean can say anything else the audio people walk in. They wave me over. "I have to go." Sean Ferro watches me walk away with my heart in my throat.

Smiling brightly at the audio people, we go over the usual stuff. They ask about music, and then we work out the details. I shut down my emotions and lock them away. I can cry tomorrow. Right now, I need to make every guy in the room think I want him and only him. I can't do that if I'm not paying attention.

My first dance of the night is always for the bachelor, who has yet to show his face, so I sit behind the curtain, waiting. Just as I think the guy is never going to show, the MC says his name. The applause echoes through the room as Peter Ferro Granz is shoved toward the stage.

The announcer's voice is filled with innuendo, but he keeps things classy. Finally, he adds, "And your brothers bought a present for you!"

Just as he says it, I step from between the slits of silver tinsel and strut straight towards Peter. Holy fuck, he looks like Jonathan. I mean, all the Ferro men have those icy blue eyes and dark hair, but Sean's crazy face is kind of off-putting. Peter isn't like that. He immediately fights back as his friends shove him into my arms.

Peter is trying to save face, but I can tell he doesn't want me anywhere near him. His toned body is stiff, like he's going to Hulk-out and smash the entire room. I smile warmly at him, giving him an out, and talk so only he can hear. "She's lucky." Everyone else is whooping because I'm bent over slightly, and they can see my ass.

He breathes like a caged animal, too fast and too hard. "What do you mean?"

"You only want her." I smile sadly at him and offer him the out. "I've never had a guy tell me no." Peter doesn't get it, not yet. I lean in and whisper in his ear. "I bet you want to strangle the guy who hired me."

"A little bit, actually." His voice is tense as he speaks, but Peter doesn't pull back. We talk quickly, as I wiggle around him, touching his shoulders and leaning into his ear way too close, smiling and winking flirtatiously.

My hair falls over my lips and I say, "You can dump the whole thing back on him without looking less manly."

He actually laughs, "Less manly?"

"Oh come on, isn't that why you let them push you down in the first place? What guy rejects a free striptease?"

Peter smiles and looks at his feet, as his friends tell him to do the kind of things a guy like him will never do. I feel the muscles in his face move against my cheek. "A guy in love."

"Yeah, like I said—she's lucky. So, this is what we do…" I whisper into his ear as I sway my hips slowly, side to side. There has to be over a hundred men in the room, all hollering at him to grope me in one way or another. As I step away from Peter, I wink at him. Lifting my hands over my head, I egg the crowd on, and encourage their catcalls and anything else I can conjure from them.

Then, I strut to the MC, grab the mic, and say in a voice that would make my mother reconsider having me, "Oh my, it's hot it here." My finger trails across my lips and down my neck. It lingers there until my hand travels over the curve of my breast and to the top corset loop. I unhook it. There are twelve to go, but that cleavage move always gets them going.

On cue, Peter grins at me and nods. He's been facing me this whole time, but he finally turns and looks back at the guys behind him. He sees his target, even though I don't. I return his wink and the guys in the room go nuts. You'd think we were having sex on the floor in front of them. I swear, men are so stupid and I'm counting on ego for this trade off.

After I wink, Peter races toward me. Raw laughter fills the hall as Peter sweeps me up in his arms. He spins me around so fast that I think my boobs are going to fly out of the bodice, but they stay put. Everyone is laughing, saying the most tawdry things they can think of. That's when I see him—Jonathan Ferro.

Peter walks over to Jon who is leaning against the wall, and thrusts me forward like a peace prize. "I owe you so much, little brother," Peter's voice booms, filling the hall without the mic. "I'll never be able to thank you accordingly, so here—have a stripper. Odds are, she'd be yours at the end of the night anyway, so it's not much of a gift, but now you don't even have to try."

Before Jonathan can say no, I'm shoved into his arms and Peter steps away. Jon's jaw is hanging open and the playboy with the stunned look on his face is enough to make everyone laugh and cheer him on. They whoop and cry out that he should take me backstage right now, while I smile and bat my eyelashes at him. I fucked up

Jon's present and I'm glad. Guys like Peter don't want me and never will, and that's the way it should be.

Jonathan's eyes dart to the side, like he wants to drop-kick me across the room. The expression is gone in a flash and replaced by one of his full wattage smiles. He gives me that sexy movie star grin the papers love so much and says, "If you insist." Without another word he takes me up to the stage, and behind the curtains as the guys roar with laughter.

CHAPTER 21

JONATHAN

The silver curtain is a joke. It doesn't give privacy at all, but it blocks the view enough that I can stop pretending that the woman in my arms isn't poison. I glare at her. "You did that on purpose."

She has the audacity to smile at me. "Maybe. How could you get a guy like Peter strippers? He would have rather had a—"

I drop her. Cassie makes that little noise that used to drive me crazy as she claws at my shirt, trying to keep her tight little body upright. Her nails scrape down my chest, and even with the shirt in the way, it's too much, reminding me of the sexy things she did—things I need to forget. Seriously, she's killing me.

I grab her wrists and yank her upright. She gasps, not expecting it, and her eyes lock with mine. "You don't know a thing about it, so don't tell me what to do." I fling her hands away like she's a piece of junk, even though I want to pull her closer.

God, I hate her. How can she look me in the eye and act like everything is fine? I want to scream at her, and at the same time, I want to pull Cassie into my arms and ask her how she ended up here, now. This is so unlike her, at least I think it is.

Maybe I don't know her at all. Maybe she was pitching shit my way from day one, but Robyn—Cassie said the same things about waiting for the right guy to Robyn. It doesn't fit into this fucked up puzzle.

Cassie rubs her wrists and glares at me. "Gee, thanks for manhandling me. I really appreciate it, jackass."

"What'd you think would happen if you came nosing around a Ferro party?"

She stares at me with those dark eyes, and that mouth—it presses together tightly like she's biting back words that she wants to hurl at my head. "I didn't know. The name on the ticket was Granz, not Ferro." Her body is tense and every time she takes a breath it looks like her breasts are going to overflow the top of her lingerie. It has

Cass cinched up so tight, making her waist too small and her breasts too big.

Trystan's voice booms from the stage and then he ducks behind the curtain. "Everything okay back here?"

I expect Cassie to have the same reaction every other woman has when Trystan Scott enters a room, but she doesn't even look at him. Her eyes are locked on me. All the things I wanted to say die in my mouth. Trystan doesn't know what she did to me, no one does.

"Fucking fabulous," I say and turn away from that stare. God, she's horrible, and beautiful.

Trystan walks over to Cassie and holds out his hand. He's lean, all taut muscle, and toned abs that are visible through his unbuttoned shirt. Traces of make-up are still on the guy's face, like he couldn't scrub it off. "Trystan Scott, Jon's best friend."

Cassie looks at his palm and grips it. "Cassie Hale, Jon's ex-friend." Trystan raises a dark eyebrow and looks over at me.

I see the questions on his face, but there's no way in hell I'm talking about it. Living through it once was enough. "She's at the top of my shitlist. She earned a permanent place of honor."

"Seriously?" Trystan looks between us and shakes his head, trying to hide a smile.

Before I know it, I'm yelling at him. Pointing to the curtain, I roar, "Get out!"

Trystan laughs, holding up his hands, palms toward me, saying, "Fine, but the guys are expecting a show. Should I tell them it's cancelled?"

Cassie shakes her head. "No, I'll work." She follows Trystan out to the stage, but I don't follow. I can't watch. Seeing her strip isn't what I want.

Sighing, I rub the heels of my hands over my face, and glance between the silvery curtains. Before I know he's there, Peter says, "So, that's Cassie Hale." I nod, staring blankly. Peter has this way of seeing the heart of the matter in a blink. I hate it, so I stand to leave but he stops me. "She's the one who was with you at the museum? The girl you protected?"

I stare into his face, wishing he wouldn't do this now. Walking away from him, I mutter, "Something like that."

Peter grabs my shoulder and steers me off the side of the stage. We head to the back of the room and for a second I think we're leaving, but then he grabs a table in the corner. "Sit."

I stand there, shoulders slumped like a slacker. I just want to get away from the thud of the bass and the blinding spotlights at the front of the room. It has nothing to do with Cassie or what's coming next—that her naked body will be displayed at the front of the room for everyone to see. The thought tries to form, but I shove it back and attempt to harden myself. I don't care. She can do whatever the fuck she wants, and it doesn't matter because I hate her. I can't stand Cassie Hale. She's a liar and she stabbed me in the back. I shouldn't give a shit what she does. My eyes flick back to the stage where she's dancing with a huge smile on her face and my fingers involuntarily turn into fists.

Yeah, I need to leave, but Peter doesn't let me. I can't be an ass to him, not after this. "Pete, I'm not in the mood."

"Neither am I, but someone went and filled my party with strippers." He smirks. "Sit."

I slip into the chair and lean back, arms folded tightly over my chest, and my head tilted to the side like I don't give a rat's ass. "Yeah, you should have seen what I had planned. It was awesome." My face lights up as I grin, which makes Peter roll his eyes.

"So, that scar on her neck—" Of course. He wants to know about Cassie.

"Was from the shrapnel." I try not to look at her, but I can't. Cassie's arms are over her head and watching her body move and sway in the light is hypnotic. I never had her. She never even kissed me, and she's stripping. It doesn't make any sense.

"Ah, so you guys match, then?" I glance up at him, not understanding his meaning. "You have matching scars. The debris hit your back. You're scar buddies?"

"She's nothing to me." My voice comes out so listless that even I don't believe me.

Peter turns his face toward the stage, watching Cassie untie the corset. Her arms are behind her back, tugging on the red strings. There's a wicked smile on her lips. My heart is pounding so fucking hard. I don't want these guys to see her. If she pulls that string and finishes unhooking the bodice... The thought grinds against everything I've ever planned to do if I saw Cassie Hale again, but I never thought it'd be under these circumstances.

A second later, Sean sits next to me. He's watching the stage with interest. "Her tits are too small, but there's something about her, isn't there Pete? With a tight little body like that, I bet her pussy is—"

My jaw locks when Sean sits down, but when he speaks—when he says those things about her—I lose it. Before I know what I'm thinking, I pull back and let my fist fly. The chairs behind us both fall to the ground. The noise and the potential for a fight make the room go quiet. All eyes are on us, looking to see what's going on. Peter watches us from his seat, but says nothing. Sean laughs and grabs my knuckles before they collide with his face. "If you want her, take her, or I will." His voice hisses in my ear as he tugs me forward and crushes my hand.

"Fine," I spit, ripping my hand out of his. "Have her."

CHAPTER 22

CASSIE

I hate this. Stop thinking. The music pounds harder and I try to stop wondering about Jon. I don't want him to see me like this. The thought makes me want to cry, but I don't leave and I don't stop. Gretchen is working the floor, staring at me with envy. I'll make more money than her tonight, just for this one little show, so it has to be hotter than hell. The club will get tons of new clients, and that means more job security for me.

The spotlights help and I'm glad they're shining in my eyes, blinding me to the crowd. I can only see the guys who are right at the edge of the stage. Swaying my hips, I move methodically, trailing my fingers over my thighs. The dance is different for each woman who does it, and since I didn't know what I was doing, I made something up. The thing is, what I made up was for Jonathan, and now he's out there somewhere, watching me.

I gasp, moving slowly, forcing my curves to work for me—bending and feeling—running my hands over my flesh until I feel hot. I used to picture Jon, sitting there watching, like it was just us. It made the routine hotter because I felt it and I was into what I was doing. My mind was far away, lost in the past. Jon was the guy I wanted, and the one I'd never have.

Any second now, I'll be standing on stage topless, wearing a G-string, and heels. And now that I have the chance to actually dance for him, I'm terrified. It's not pretend anymore, it's a horrible mistake and I want to stop. But I can't. I'm trapped. There are too many bills, too many people that I owe money to for me to stop. I can't.

Lowering myself, I squat and slowly open my knees. Tilting my head back, I trail my fingers to the V between my legs and up my corset to my neck, finally slipping them into my mouth. I feel the men's lust filled eyes on me, and their desire. The room has grown quiet as they watch and want me.

I stand and stretch my hands over my head and when I look out, I can't see Jon. This is it. Reaching behind my back for the corset strings, I pull. The fabric loosens and I can breathe again, but there's not enough air. Not here, not now. My lips part as I feel the bodice slip slightly, and my fingers start to work on the front closure, unhooking it and revealing the soft skin beneath. I stare into the crowd, barely breathing, wishing to God that I was somewhere else.

Another hook pops open and the corset is ready to fall to the floor. It's held in place by a couple of hooks and nothing more. That's when a loud boom comes from the back of the room. Two men are standing, and someone throws a punch. All the guys turn and I freeze in place when I see who it is. The house lights come up slightly, enough to see Sean and Jon.

I can't hear them, but Jon storms out without looking my way.

That's when things get really weird. It takes a few minutes for things to settle back down. The houselights dim and the music gets cranked up louder. I shove every thought out of my head and try to finish my striptease. My hand unhooks one loop, and then another, so my hand is the only thing holding up the bodice. The corset is ready to slip off. All I have to do is remove my hand, but I hesitate. My stomach is in knots and I feel like I'm going to puke. I'm taking too long, I know I am. Covering my fear with a fake smile, I force my hand away. That's when a man rushes me. I feel hard abs slap against my skin, as my corset hits the floor. I shriek before I see who it is.

Jonathan.

I'm nearly naked and his body is pressed against mine, his arms around me, hiding my body. He looks into my face, breathing hard, and says, "I can't let you do this."

Bruce is swearing up a storm, shoving his way through the room to get to me, but the guys are blocking his path. They're cheering for Jon, acting like he does crazy shit like this all the time.

My heart pounds violently as I look into his face. "Jon, I have to."

"No you don't." He scoops me up into his arms, angling my body towards his, and spots Bruce.

"Put her the fuck down!" The man is beyond scary. There's death in Bruce's eyes as he plows through the crowd like a rabid bull.

Jon laughs like he planned this, and then sprints off with me in his arms. I cling, afraid that he'll drop me. Jon bursts through the side door and runs down a hallway, and then down another. He shoulders his way into a room and slams the door. His chest fills with air rapidly as he tries to catch his breath with me still in his arms. After a second he looks at me, but his gaze won't meet mine. He presses his eyes closed tight, like he knows he's messed up.

Every inch of me is trembling, and no matter how hard I try to make it stop, I can't. My body shivers in his arms. When his eyes open, he looks at me. "I'm sorry."

"It's all right. I was stalling. I couldn't..." my voice catches in my throat. I couldn't strip in front of him, but he's holding me in his arms and the only reason he can't see my breasts is because I'm turned into his chest with my arms around his neck. Tears sting in my eyes, so I look down and hide my face.

We're in a room that smells like leather and old books. Everything is richly colored browns and reds. There are a few seating areas with scattered sofas and tables. Heavy velvet drapes hang floor to ceiling, making the room feel warm and lush.

"You're cold." He sets me down, careful not to look, and grabs a blanket off the couch behind us. Heart thumping fast, I cover my chest with my hands. As Jon steps toward me, his eyes wander over my body and make me flush. He wraps the blanket around my shoulders, pausing for a second to look into my eyes. I think he's going to say something when his lips part, but he doesn't. Instead, his hands drop and he steps away.

"Thank you."

Jon nods for a moment and then laughs, but there's no joy in it. "Sean played me. Holy fuck, I'm a moron." His laughter turns genuine as he circles the room and then stops in front of me.

Bruce screams my name from somewhere down the hall. I don't answer him. "It's okay, you got me off the stage. There was no other way for me to back out. Thank you." Glancing at the carpet, I clutch the front of the blanket tighter.

"Why'd you do it?" My eyes drift up and meet his. For a moment, I think he's asking about the reporters all those years ago, but he's not. He's asking about tonight. "Why'd you take this job?"

"I had to." I don't elaborate. The lump in my throat is strangling me. I can barely breathe.

"What about your ideals? How can you do this if you actually believed what you told me before..." *Before you turned on me. Before you sold me out...* Those are the words he doesn't say, but I hear them all the same. Jon runs his hand through his hair.

Bruce's voice is growing louder. He'll find us any second.

I smile sadly at Jon. "I did believe what I told you. I was waiting for the right guy."

"And you found him?"

The way he stares at me makes the center of my chest ache. I don't want to say it, but I have to. I try to force my lips into a smile, but it looks like I'm going to cry. I nod, still watching his eyes. "Yeah, I found him."

CHAPTER 23

JONATHAN

I stand there and gape. I know I only have seconds to talk before that thug comes barreling through the door, but it's all I can do. She found him—Cassie found Mr. Wonderful—and gave away her first kiss and everything else, but somehow she's working at a club, stripping for money. The guy must be a total asshole.

I want to scream. This can't be happening. My heart twists inside my chest, but that's impossible because she already ripped it out. But I feel it. I still react to her, to those deliciously dark eyes, and that hypnotic voice. I want to wrap my arms around her and start over, but we can't. We aren't the same people anymore. Besides, Mr. Assface is probably sitting at home waiting for her. Cassie has a life and I'm not part of it. The whole thing pisses me off.

This is a million miles from where she wanted to be, and I know it.

Barely keeping my temper in check, I ask, "So you found him? And he lets you do this? Work parties? Strip? Maybe even take a guy on the side?" Her shoulders tense as I verbally bitchslap her. Cassie's red lips part and I see the hurt in her eyes, that is, before it's replaced by anger and her hand flying toward my face. It connects with my cheek, stinging the flesh, but I don't move. I stare at her, wondering how she fell so far, so fast.

Cassie breathes hard, her body shaking as her temper flares back to life. "You don't know a damn thing about me, so don't pretend to even give a shit, Ferro." She's in my face, hissing at me in that lethal tone I remember so well. Last time she scolded me like this it was because I provoked her. Maybe I did the same thing this time, maybe I'm not ready to let her rip my heart out twice. It's funny how I thought I was dead inside until I heard her voice again. Cassie Hale is the defibrillator for my fucked up heart. Seeing her again shocked the hell out of me and I'm suddenly so much more than a walking corpse.

Bruce's crazed screams get closer. Doors slam up and down the hall. There are seconds left, and that's it. There isn't another minute with her, and the funny part is that this is nothing like I imagined. I always thought that if I saw Cassie Hale on the street again that I'd verbally rip her to shreds because of what she did to me. So it's strange standing here, watching her tremble, and wanting to pull her into my arms and save her from this shit.

No. She's not my problem, not anymore. But the way she looks at me from under those dark lashes, the way the lights cast a dim glow on her perfect face, and the way she clutches the blanket to her throat like it's a goddamn lifejacket and she's drowning—it's too much. I can't step away. I can't leave her alone to endure whatever fate she's been handed, even if she deserves it.

Pressing my lips together, I step toward her, taking her shoulders in my hands. She stiffens in my arms and it's nothing like before. She doesn't trust me, not anymore.

Too many things happened between us. It doesn't matter that I saved her life once. That was a lifetime ago, and that version of Cassie Hale is long gone. But she's not completely lost, is she?

As our eyes drift and our gazes lock, I see her still in there, hidden beneath the fray. I lift a hand and touch the ends of her glitter-caked hair. "I wanted you to find him. Even after everything—I hoped you'd get the life you wanted, the man that was right for you. You meant something to me once. I won't pretend you didn't, which is why I can't fathom you being here, now. You said you found him? Then where is he, Cass?"

Fuck, she looks like she's going to cry. The bottoms of her eyelids flutter and her gaze darts away from mine, but I take her chin in my hand and draw it back. Come on, Cass, tell me what happened to you.

Her lips part, but she can't speak. An awful look floods her eyes as her brows wrinkle together. My hand slips away and Cassie tightens her hold on the blanket. I see her fingers clenching it so tightly that her bright pink nails bite through the weave. She wasn't the kind of girl to wear pink or do her nails with those fake plastic things. Cassie was real, every last part of her.

"It's not what you think. He—" before she can finish her sentence, the door flies open.

Bruce has a terrifying look on his face—he's pissed. The insane rhino of a man rushes at me. His shoulder hits my side at the same time that his fist finds my face. Shit. I'm done talking. All the anger that's been coursing through me comes out in a fury. My fists connect with his freakishly large body over and over again. Something cracks and I hear Cassie screaming in the background, but we don't stop.

Bruce would have snapped me in half by now if I didn't know how to fight, but anger is clouding my judgment. Bruce spits at me as I launch myself at him, grabbing his neck and locking him in place. "You stupid little shit," he huffs, and rank air fills my face. The guy has alcohol on his breath.

I squeeze harder as Bruce slams me into a wall. The force of the impact nearly knocks me loose, but I hold on. Suddenly I notice that there are people there, besides the thug, Cassie, and me, but we don't stop. Using my weight, I manage to throw him off balance and slam his head into a bookcase. The shelf cracks and the contents fall to the floor along with him. When he pushes himself up, a bead of blood trickles into his eye. He leaves it there and gives me a look that says he's going to kill me.

Suddenly, I see who else is in the room. Trystan and Bryan flank one side of me, and Peter and Sean flank the other. Sean is the one who speaks. "Come and get him." Then, I feel Sean's foot in my back, shoving me forward.

I thought they had my back, but when I look at my brothers they both seem pissed. "This is your mess, Jonny."

Trystan steps forward and shoots Sean a disgusted look. "Some brother."

"Fuck you, Scott, you goddamn parasite," Sean bites back.

Trystan flips Sean off and remains at my side. Bryan is a messed up motherfucker because he's laughing like this is funny. He steps next to me and smirks at Bruce after folding his arms over his chest like he thinks this will be fun. Sometimes I wonder about Bryan. The man doesn't seem to value his life, like at all, but all the same, I'm glad he's standing next to me right now.

Then everything changes because the manager of this beautiful building storms into the room, screaming at the top of his lungs about damages and cops. His face is bright red and the little veins on his temples are throbbing like they're going to blow. Shit.

Bryan lets out a huff of air and turns toward the guy, annoyed. "You called the cops? What the fuck is wrong with you, man? You have the richest men in New York standing in your building, along with the rock star over there," he jabs his thumb at Trystan, "and you decide to call the cops? You're going about it wrong, man. You need to call the press." Bryan looks over at Bruce. It's clear he plans to patch things up with the manager if Bruce is ready to let it drop. "Are we done here? Or do I need to stick around, because no one fucks with Jonny Ferro."

Bruce looks like a beast, his massive body straining, muscles tense to the point they're going to snap. He points at me and snarls, "You're not welcome at my club. If you ever show your face there again, I'll rip it off."

CHAPTER 24

CASSIE

Bryan Ferro wasn't kidding. The press showed up in a blaze of flashing lights and endless questions. The entire thing gave everyone what they wanted. Well, almost everyone. Jon is going to be the one to take all the blame. He accepted it graciously. While I ducked out the back door, Jon walked out the front, right into the eye of the storm.

The headlines this morning are not kind. The press took every slant you could possibly imagine, and each one made the Ferro's look worse than the last. Beth tosses me another paper. "That one is going to be trouble."

I glance up at her. Beth is wearing a cute little sweat suit with a white tee shirt and running shoes. It's her day off garb. There isn't a stitch of make-up on her face and her hair is swept up into a ponytail. She looks pretty this way. Sometimes it feels like we're leading double lives, but that would be a lot more exciting. Beth is just working her way through school, and me, well, I'm hiding.

I take the paper and flip it open to the page that's dog-eared. There's a small picture of Jon carrying me. It must have been taken before things went to hell last night, before Bruce found us. I stare at it. My face is perfectly clear. A chill works its way up my spine as I stare, unblinking, with my mind racing.

"Someone must have snuck in a camera," I say. Beth sits down next to me on the old couch. This little basement apartment suddenly feels too small. The lack of windows never bothered me, but now I can't breathe. I rush across the room, throw open the door, and take the short flight of stairs two at a time, running outside. Cold air hits my face and I stop, doubling over and holding my knees, while I breathe.

Beth is there a second later. Her hand is on my back. "He might not even see it."

Bruce was my safety net, my reason for taking the stripper job in the first place. The night they hired me, I accepted the job with one condition—they can't let my husband inside. I handed Bruce his picture and, so far, it's been quiet. I've kept my head down and Bruce makes sure I can work in peace. The other jobs didn't last long. I'd get fired when my husband would show up. Mark would scream at me like a deranged customer. When I explained who he was and what he was doing, it didn't matter— the end result was the same every time. Gather your things and go. No one wants family drama in their business. No one wants to think about what a guy like that does to a girl like me when we get home. It's not a nice thought, even though it's glaringly obvious. I've been fired too many times, and not having a source of income is an issue since I need a place to live and food to eat. I'm on my own and have been for a while.

Then I met Beth. She needed a roommate and had this little apartment in Bay Shore, not far from Sunrise Highway. Drug dealers live in the house across the street, but our landlord is nice. She's a little old lady that can't pay her taxes unless she rents out the basement, and she likes us. Mrs. McKinzey doesn't comment on our clothes when we leave for work. She probably thinks we're lesbians since we never have any men over. She bought this house new and lived here while the neighborhood went to hell around her. Beth treats her like the mother she never had.

The guys across the street are sitting in their shiny new Caddy with the bass blasting. I shouldn't look at them. I should go back inside, but I can't. It feels like my lungs are being crushed. Mark. If he finds me again, oh God, I don't even want to think about it. One of the guys across the street shoots me a nasty look. His skin is bronzed and there's a goatee cut into sharp lines around his mouth. Loose pants hang off his hips, but it's that tank top that lets me see all his tats and ripped muscles. He's younger than I am. We stare at each other. I know I should look away, but I can't.

"Oh shit." Beth glances across the street in time to see the guy walking straight at us. He doesn't have a leisurely pace, and everything about him makes me want to duck back inside, but I can't move. Some part of my brain—the crazy part—is tired of being pushed around. I don't want to hide from anyone anymore.

The man crosses the street and is in our yard. He walks straight up to us, and I don't move. I'm still gasping for air like a beached whale. "Is she okay?"

Beth blinks. That was the last thing I expected him to say, and apparently Beth thinks so too. "Uh, yeah. She's got asthma and lost her inhaler. I told her to come out here and get some air. It'll pass."

Her lie fits with my ragged breaths. The man reaches into his pocket and Beth tenses. If he stabs me, I hope he goes for my throat. He can connect the dots on my scar. The shrapnel almost cut deep enough to kill me. Almost. Sometimes I wish it did.

When he steps closer, my heart races harder. Beth starts to say something, but the guy shoves his fist in front of my face and opens his palm. There's an inhaler in his hand. "Here, take it. I've got another one." When I don't move, he makes an annoyed sound, shakes it, and takes the cover off. "I didn't even use it, yet. Take it. The ER visit for this kinda shit is nearly five grand. Believe me, I know."

I take the thing and use it. Straightening, I look at the guy. His dark skin is perfectly smooth. He smiles at me, revealing a gold cap with a diamond set on his front tooth. "Feel better?"

I nod. "Yeah, thank you."

"I'm Kam. I own the house across the street. If you ever need anything, an egg, cup of sugar, an inhaler—whatever—come over. I try to stay off Ms. McKinzey's lawn. The crazy old bat has a gun in there." Kam says it like he doesn't have one shoved down his pants, but I can see the hilt under his shirt.

I nod. "This is Beth and I'm Cassie. Thanks for this." I hold up the inhaler, meaning to give it back, but Kam steps away, shoving his hands into his pockets.

"Nah, you keep that. You might need it again." He turns on his heel and returns to the guys in the Caddy parked on his driveway.

Beth flicks her gaze my way. "That was weird."

"Yeah, it was." We're both staring at the house that no one looks at. "He's afraid of Ms. McKinzey."

"Yeah, I caught that. As if life wasn't strange enough, right?"

I nod slowly. Kam glances at us and smirks. I wave at him, bending the tips of my fingers once, before turning to go back inside. "I think we just made friends with an asthmatic drug lord."

Beth squeals and claps her hands together. "Ooh! I'll have to write about it in my diary."

"Crazy white girl."

"Right back at you, pasty."

CHAPTER 25

JONATHAN

Lying in bed isn't going to delay the inevitable. First, Pete's fiancé, Sidney, is going to kill me, and then when she's done Mom will take care of the body. Awesome. I dress, pulling on my favorite pair of jeans and then a blue shirt that I swore I'd never wear again. Cassie gave it to me that summer we were in Mississippi. I'm a pussy for still having it, but I was never able to throw the damn thing out. I slip it over my head and layer it with a button down. After running some gel through my hair, I head to the dining room. When I get there, it's empty. There's no trace of anyone, which is strange. This can't be good.

My head throbs as I walk around the massive table and take my seat. There's a sideboard filled with hot food hidden beneath silver domes, but I'm not particularly hungry. Instead, I pour a cup of coffee and sit back in my chair, wondering what happened to Cassie. I haven't forgiven her for what she did, but I'm not such a dick that I can ignore her now. Stupid ideas bounce through my head that lead back to Cassie's club and Bruce's fists. I can't look for her there. I need to try and find her another way first. I pull out my phone and type her name into the search bar of the web browser.

My eyes flick up when I feel slender fingers slip over my shoulders. Turning the phone face down, I put it on the table before she can see.

"Good morning, Jonathan." Her voice is liquid heat and utterly inappropriate, but that's never stopped her before. Chrissy's hands linger on my shoulders before working their way down my chest, stopping at my nipples, circling them with her long nails. "I thought we had plans last night." I try to glance at her, but Chrissy has her face pressed against mine. Her warm breath tickles my ear when she speaks. "Maybe you're wanting something else—that's all right. You can go do whoever you want, but at the end of the day, I know it's me that you really want." She squeezes my nipples once, hard. The sensation shoots straight to my groin even though I'm mentally somewhere else.

Chrissy is Dad's latest toy, but she's managed to stick around longer than the last one. She has dark blonde hair that falls in a shiny sheet half way down her back, amazing hips, and a boob job that almost makes them look and feel real. She presses those oversized melons to my cheek before standing and walking around the table to her seat. She's my age and wearing a bikini that barely covers anything. My mother is going to flip out. When we were younger, we were sent away from the table for coming down without shoes on, and here's Chrissy with her nipples barely covered. The sarong draped over her hip is sheer and does nothing to hide her perfect ass or the tiny scrap of fabric covering it.

Chrissy doesn't ask questions because she doesn't care. Her goal is to marry a Ferro. I know this because she told me while we were fucking. She'll do anything I want, any time I ask, and even some times when I don't. Before I left last night, I thought I'd want her, but after I saw Cassie I didn't feel like being with anyone. I'm not going to be celibate. I'm not stupid, but why screw someone if you don't feel like it?

Chrissy smiles at me and leans forward slightly, while taking her bikini top between her fingers. She lifts the fabric and flashes me, then winks as she tucks her tits back out of sight. The other mistresses were afraid of my mother and did everything possible to not get caught messing around with me, but Chrissy is pushing the line. It's like she wants to have my parents walk in on us fucking on the breakfast table. That doesn't sound half bad, and yesterday morning I was so pissed that I would have, but I've got some sense of self-preservation. I might be the heir, but Mom can still disown me. Without the Ferro name, I have nothing.

Sean walks in next wearing dark jeans and a black sweater. He looks like the grim reaper with a scowl on his face. He says nothing, doesn't look at either of us, and picks up the paper. Peter and Sidney are the next to show up. They walk in, hand in hand, smiling.

As soon as Sidney lifts her gaze and sees me, the happiness washes away and I get snapped at. "You and I need to talk, Jonathan."

"Told you she'd be pissed," Sean says from behind his paper.

"You said Pete would be pissed, not Sidney."

"Same difference. The man only thinks with her pussy now. He's whipped." Sean places his coffee cup down and looks over the top of his paper when no one answers. Sidney's mouth is hanging open, Peter's scowling at him, Chrissy looks aroused, and I'm laughing because his decorum is so messed up. The guy has no idea he said anything offensive, or maybe he just acts that way. "What? We're going to lie about it?"

Peter glares at Sean, who is sitting next to Chrissy. "You're going to treat Sidney with respect."

"I *am* treating her with respect. You're the one I have the problem with." Sean goes back to reading his paper. Chrissy slurps her coffee and makes a high pitched squeal because it's too hot. Sean glances at her. "If our mother doesn't kill you for wearing that to the table, then I'm going to do it. Act like a fucking adult if you want to be in this room."

Chrissy's eyes fill with fire. She hates Sean. Everyone hates Sean. Before she can say anything, Bryan walks through the door. He's half dressed, wearing a pair of wrinkled jeans and an equally wrinkled shirt.

I raise my chin his way and say, "Did Aunt Lizzy throw you out?"

Bryan sits down hard next to me and grabs his napkin. As he places it in his lap, he glances my way and says, "Did you see the papers? They had a shot of me, you, and Scott all standing there with the word STRIPPERS in the headline. What do you think?"

Mom's voice is utterly cold when she speaks. "I think my sister is right and we should castrate the lot of you." Her eyes lock on mine, furious. The thing with Mom's anger is that she hides it. The only way to tell that she's more pissed than usual is the tiny wrinkle between her Botoxed eyebrows. It twitches in and out, like an old television show with poor reception. Mom turns her gaze on Chrissy and snaps her fingers at the girl. "You, get out."

Chrissy frowns. Her mouth opens, ready to make an argument, but mother doesn't stop snapping. "I've had enough problems with my family and sluts to last a few days. I'm normally a patient woman, but if you don't have the decency to show up at my table, with my family, and wear pants, then I don't owe you a shred of respect. Get out." Mom's voice growls those last two words.

Chrissy's eyes narrow, like she's thinking about fighting back, but she doesn't. Instead, she takes her mimosa and storms out of the room. Dad brushes past Chrissy, his old eyes sweeping over her young, tight body, as she pushes her way to the pool.

"Chrissy?" he calls after her, but she doesn't stop.

Dad turns and storms into the room. Wonderful. World War 7, or 9, or whatever the hell we're up to. Slouching in my chair, I wait. One day they'll all kill each other and I can eat alone.

"What did you say to her?" he yells at Mom.

"Merely that she shouldn't rest her breasts on the table. Clothing is not optional. Honestly, does she think we're running a brothel?" Mom's eyes cut to me, and then Bryan. "Certainly not, although the boys have made it rather unclear, recently. Care to explain yourselves?" She glares at us.

Bryan pushes back from the table to stand, but never gets to his feet. Mom gives him that deadly smile of hers, and says, "Elisabeth told me that you ran out before she could talk to you, so I volunteered to take care of you both."

"Shit," Bryan mutters, and goes pale.

"Until you can act like reasonable young men, your allowances are suspended. Bryan, you're not getting a cent of Ferro money for the next month. Jonathan, I expect you to come into the office and work. No more laying around the pool and screwing anything that washes up." She gives my Dad a disapproving look, and then returns her death stare my way. "Keep it in your pants."

Bryan slumps next to me like he's been shot. There's more coming, we both know it, and that's going to be the worst part. However, Mom doesn't say it right then. She sips her coffee and turns her fangs on Pete and Sean. "And you two—where were you when all this was going on?" Peter tries to talk, but Mom cuts him off. "You expect to keep your job when you show up in the papers with a stripper on your lap? And you," all her venom is directed at Sean, "you know better than this. You should have kept it from happening. You're not the man I thought you were, Sean."

Sean stares at her, expressionless. He doesn't apologize or hang his head the way the rest of us do. No, he looks at her like she just commented on the weather. "Likewise, Mother."

Holy fuck. He did not just say that. Me, Peter, Sidney and Bryan lean forward. We can't help it. Somehow we ended up in the front row seats to the apocalypse. The two of them—Mom and Sean—are so alike, but neither of them sees it, and they'll both fight to the death.

Mother's lips twist into a smile that looks utterly amused. "You think I'm not pulling my weight? Ask me what I was doing last night while the four of you had nipples in your faces?" She glances at Sidney, "Sorry for being so crass dear, but I doubt it offends someone of your stature anyway." Sidney doesn't respond. Instead, Peter's hand covers hers and pins it to the table. It's a silent plea for her to keep her mouth closed. But, Mom isn't watching, or doesn't care—probably the latter—and turns her venom back to Sean. "Ask me, Sean. Ask me where all the pictures of you and Peter are, and why not a single one was published?"

"Buying pictures won't hide what happened there," Sean says flatly.

"A picture is more damning than anything else. It's physical proof that you were doing something you should not have done. The four of you smear the Ferro name, and waste the influence you were given—"

Sean laughs, like he's happy, even though he's angrier than I've seen him in a long time. "I waste nothing—not time, not money, not stature, and certainly not my morning by sitting here with company as rancid as you. Enjoy your breakfast, Mother." Sean stands and leaves before another word is said, which leaves the rest of us as open targets.

If she's hurt, Mother doesn't show it. She ignores Dad and eats in silence. When she leaves, a hand smacks the back of my head. When I turn, Sidney's standing behind me, her face level with mine. "If you ever drop a naked girl in Peter's lap again, I'll cut off your balls and hang them on my Christmas tree. Is that clear enough for you?"

Bryan stifles a laugh, but Peter jabs his ribs with his elbow anyway, then stands and takes Sidney's hand. "Crystal clear. He gets it. Come on, Sid." But she pulls away.

"No, he doesn't get it! The wedding is three weeks away and he's acting like a goddamn child! I don't want this Peter. I don't want your name dragged through the mud. I don't want your mother lording it over you whenever you mess up, and I don't want your little brother making things worse when they're already hard enough."

Sidney's angry eyes are burning holes into the side of my face. "What were you thinking? You gave him an education and a job, and then threw strippers and paparazzi at him? Tell me how that was supposed to work out, Jonathan, because I don't see it."

"It's what guys normally do—" I try to apologize, but she won't let me.

"Yeah, but you guys aren't normal. Everyone is looking at you, watching you, and hoping to God that you screw up so they have a story to run in tomorrow's paper! Jon, I care about you, I really do, but you can't keep doing stuff like this." Sidney's voice shakes and I know there are tears on her face. I don't look at her. I can't.

Peter pulls her from the room and I slink down in my chair, feeling like a piece of shit.

CHAPTER 26

CASSIE

The week passes quietly, for which I'm grateful. If Mark had showed up I'd have to pick up everything and move again, and I'm sick of moving. This is the longest I've been able to stay anywhere and it's nice. Well, for the most part it's nice. I look down at my bra and panty set, wishing that I didn't have to do this. I was so close, so fucking close to getting what I wanted. I had the perfect guy, the nice little house with a new car in the driveway, and then it all went to hell.

I'm not naïve anymore, I know I never had any of that stuff, but the illusion was nice while it lasted. Now, every moment is hell. If a creditor isn't hounding me for cash, then the repo guy is chasing me, trying to get my car, which is currently hidden in Mrs. McKinzey's garage. The sad part is that the mountain of debt isn't even mine, it's Mark's. I didn't do this, but I'm the one paying for it. I'm a college dropout, hiding in the 'hood, biding my time, so that I can earn enough money to get a second chance at life. Assuming I can avoid Mark in the meantime.

"Cassie, you're on stage next. Get out here!" I'm not Bruce's favorite person after last weekend, but he doesn't blame me. The boss found out, of course. The pictures in the paper made it clear that someone grabbed me, a Ferro, and that Bruce didn't or couldn't do his job. He would have been fired if I didn't speak up, but Bruce doesn't know that. I went to Jeff's office alone and explained to the owner that Bruce wasn't to blame. Jeff said I didn't get it, and still planned on firing his ass, so I said I'd pay Bruce's salary to give him another chance. The guy might be a thug, but he has a kid at home. I can't be the reason why he got fired, and if I wasn't the girl stripping that night, none of it would have happened.

The week is almost over. Maybe it was stupid, especially since Bruce has no idea who's paying his wages this week, but I can't be the reason someone falls apart. I already was once, and the mess I saw in Jon

Ferro's eyes last weekend made me sick. I caused it, I know I did.

Yanking my garters in place, I dust myself with some glitter and head out to the stage. My entire outfit is cotton candy pink. It matches the pink room, the one spot in the club that isn't filled with wall to wall guys. There's usually a handful of men in there, because they are the only ones who can afford it. I feel better about taking my clothes off since I'll never see them again, and there aren't as many of them. Guys like that don't hang out at places like this. They tend to be the CEO types that had an argument with their perfect wife. They blow off steam down here, and then disappear again.

I enter the room from backstage and peer through the pale pink curtain. The entire area is champagne pink, with bits of sparkle. It looks hideous with the lights all the way up, but with flickering candlelight and a single spotlight on me, it has a serene feel. The music starts and I strut out on stage, moving my body to the music, not paying attention to who's out there. I never look at their faces. My eyes don't even connect with their bodies, usually gazing just above their heads. It makes it less real, like they aren't real people and I'm not really doing this. Eye contact shatters the illusion.

Bruce has his arms folded across his chest and watches me from the back of the room. His phone is out. He looks at the screen and smiles, before tucking it away. His kid took her first steps tonight and he's beaming, telling everyone, showing them the video of his little princess and her wobbly legs.

As I make my way to the pole, I glance around the room. There are only a couple of guys here tonight, which is weird for a weekend. They're both sitting away from the stage, back in the corners. I plaster a smile on my face and start my dance, thinking of Jonathan and the things I wish he'd done to me when we were younger. Sweat makes my body glisten as I work, splaying my legs, and rubbing my hands over my slick body with my eyes half closed. The bra comes off, and gets tossed to the side, showing my taut nipples. I swing on the pole, tossing my hair around, and breathing hard before stripping completely.

Then the show gets more intense. I touch places on my body that I shouldn't touch in public, while tossing my head back and staring at the ceiling. I reach above my head with my hands and stretch, forcing my breasts higher, and making my waist slimmer, before I push my ankles apart. My hands drift down my arms, to my head, following my long curls to my breasts, and then to the V in my legs. I gasp and wink, followed by a wicked smile. I hold the pose until the spot turns off.

The money is made in the next part of the night, but with only two guys, damn— I'll barely make enough money to pay Bruce. Beth is going to kill me if I don't clear at least my share of gas money. I slip back into my outfit and head out to the floor. Music pulses through the small room. I need to concentrate on what I'm doing because it takes a lot of finesse, but my mind keeps drifting to Jon.

I shove my life away, cramming it back into the back of my head as I approach a young man sitting in one of the corners. I don't look at his face, I never do.

"Hey, baby."

"Hey yourself," he says holding up a hundred dollar bill, which is the only kind of bill you can use in the pink room. There's an insanely high cover charge, which goes to the boss, but I get to keep the money I make on the floor. I take it from him and slip it into my G string. I don't look at his face as I work him over. He keeps handing me bills, so I stay and dance for him until he's done with me.

The music cues me back to the stage, where I do another striptease, this one much raunchier than the first. By the time I'm done, the gentlemen in the corner is gone, but two more have taken his place. They wave bills at me, but I pass them and head to the man who's been here since I stepped out on stage.

My thoughts roam to that secret place in the back of my mind where there are no emotions, just darkness and shadows. I don't want to think about what I'm doing or how I got here. Doing that is like dumping lighter fluid over my head. One spark will burn me to a crisp in a matter of seconds. No one starts out life this way. No girl ever dreams of being a stripper when she grows up, and thinking about what I am, what I've become, only makes it worse. So I don't think at all. I'm lost somewhere within my mind, where no one can touch me, where I'm safe.

"Hey, baby," I say, my eyes looking anywhere but his face.

"Hey, Cassie."

His voice jars me, slamming me back into reality with a deafening thud. Shivers course through my skin, freezing me in place as my heart explodes in my chest. "Jonathan?"

CHAPTER 27

JONATHAN

I hate sitting and watching her work the other guy. Every bit of me wants to strut over to the man and slam my fist down his throat, but I manage to wait my turn. Barely. Maybe this was a stupid idea, and I know my mother will kill me when she finds out, but I had to do it. I couldn't let things go on this way, not for Cassie. It doesn't matter what she did to me back then, I can't wish this on her. Based on the look on her face the other night, she doesn't enjoy this job at all.

Maybe showing up here wasn't a good idea, but I can't leave now. She's walking over to me with a sexy smile on her face. Her body shimmers like she's made of stardust, her hips swaying to the music as she walks toward me, and the old dreams of squeezing that perfect ass hit me hard. I still want her. How could I? The woman nearly ruined me, and I'm still drooling like a love struck teenager.

Cassie's dark hair hangs in loose curls over her pale skin. That body is so overwhelmingly beautiful that I can't look away. My palms grow hot, followed by the rest of my body. She'll think I have no pride. She'll slap me, and rip my heart out of my chest, again. But only if I let her, and that's not why I'm here. As much as I'd love a lap dance from this bewitching woman, I want something else much more.

Her voice isn't right. She doesn't sound like herself when she speaks, but when I reply, oh God… Those startling dark eyes flash with recognition. She glares at me like she hates me, but I don't move. The smug smile remains on my face as I lean back in my chair.

I hold up a few bills, not really thinking about how I'm going to tell her. I just need her to stay by me for a second. "Dance for me, Cass."

Her lower lip trembles ever so slightly before she reaches for the money. The expression on her face tells me this is the equivalent of kicking her in the stomach.

I'm a dick. I should stop her right now, and tell her why I'm here, but I can't resist the urge to give her a little bit of the hell that I lived through because of her. Cassie tucks the bills into her panty and steps closer. Raising my hands, palms out, I say, "Stop. From there's fine."

The insult washes the life out of her eyes and her shoulders slump. It's only a second, but I see it—I know what I did to her—but I can't stop. Cassie lifts her arms above her head and starts to sway her hips. Her ass comes close to my face, but I don't move. She dances and I let her. Every time she stops, I shove another bill at her. I must have given her over a grand by now, but I don't care. When she reaches for the money this time, I lean in and say, "Allow me."

Cassie stiffens and nods once, then forces a hip my way. I lift the satin of her panty and tuck the bill in place before looking up into her face. Too many unspoken words pass between us. I spare her the final dance and stand. With those stripper heels on her feet, we're eye to eye. "Why'd you do it? I would have done anything for you, Cassie, and you ruined me."

Her dark eyes fall to the floor as her breathing becomes rough, like she's trying not to cry. But when she looks back up at me, she doesn't offer an explanation. There are no words, no apologies rolling off her lips. If she told me why, if she said anything, I could forgive her—I could— because I so desperately need her. But Cassie doesn't say anything.

Instead she hangs her head and tucks a dark curl behind her ear. "I have to go."

I nod, and now we're both looking at the floor. Her toenails are painted, each one tipped with silver sparkles. "So do I."

I lose my nerve. I don't tell her what I came in for, or what it means to her. Instead, I slip out before she remembers that I've been banished from this place. Bruce was supposed to carve me a new face if I tried to come in here again, but his new boss wouldn't allow it.

As I leave the pink room, I run my hand over the back of my neck and expel the perfumed air like poison. I run into a thin girl—the one that was wrestling with

Cassie the other night at the party—Beth. She looks up at me in shock, and says, "Is it true? Did you really buy this place?"

I smirk at her and nod. "Yeah, I did. Welcome to Club Ferro."

CHAPTER 28

CASSIE

"He didn't," I say to Beth, my jaw hanging open as I look at the pile of cash in my hand. "Jon bought the club? He actually said that?"

Beth nods as she pulls off her thigh highs. "Yeah, he said it's going to be Club Ferro. I didn't really get a chance to talk to him, but that's why he was here tonight. Apparently, he bought the club this afternoon and came in tonight to tour the building when it was in use and sign the papers." Beth isn't stupid. She's been chattering to keep my head from exploding.

I can't work for him. I could barely deal with Jon at the party, but seeing him every day—here—oh God. It feels like someone dropped my heart down a mine shaft and I'm going to puke. A thin sheen of sweat covers my face as I lean forward in my chair in the dressing room.

Gretchen glares at me. "If you get us sick, I swear to God—"

"She's not sick, so go suck it, evil whore," Beth snaps back.

Gretchen places her hands on her hips. She's standing there in her cotton bra and panty set, almost dressed to leave, and glares at us. "At least I don't live in a hole like you two lesbians."

"Go fuck yourself, Gretchen." Beth snaps back.

"Why don't you make me, Beth?" The two of them are standing toe to toe, two seconds away from a cat fight. I glance around for Bruce, but he's not here.

Standing suddenly, I shove my way between them. "Go kiss up to the new boss. Odds are you'll get my job if he likes you."

Beth gives me a weird look, but Gretchen doesn't contain her excitement. "Already started, bitch. Guess who's taking me home tonight?" Jon offered to take her home? My head spins and I blink it away, trying not to jump to conclusions, but it can only mean one thing. I hate the idea of the two of them sleeping together. No. This can't happen.

I lose it.

I've only lost control of myself twice in my life, prior to this moment. Once was when I was nine years old and Jennifer Malby stole one of my earrings and said it was hers. She grinned at me as she fastened it on the lapel of her denim jacket, knowing that she'd never have to give it back. Her smug look pushed me over the top, so I punched her in the face and took my earring back. The second time was at the grocery store. Some woman hit me in the head with crap that was sticking out of her cart and told me to watch where I was going, like it was my fault. I took her broom and hurled it down the aisle before giving her the biggest bitch-out she'd ever seen. Both of those times, I'd been under so much pressure that I couldn't take it anymore, and so I lashed out at the next poor bastard who decided to screw with me when I had no capacity to deal with it.

There's nothing in my mind telling me to stop. I throw the first punch and then we're a flurry of flying fists and pulling hair.

Screams and nasty things come from my mouth, but I don't stop until I have the bitch pinned to the floor. My arm winds back to punch her in the face when a strong hand yanks me away and pulls me up off the floor.

"What the hell are you doing?" Jon snaps at me, as he separates us.

Bruce is suddenly there as well and won't let Gretchen near me. He arrived a second after Jon and yanked the slut to her feet. "Go simmer down," he scolds her and points to a chair in the corner.

Jon still has a hold of my arm. He glares around the room and says in a tone that makes me afraid, "Anyone who fights like this will be fired. No exceptions. Am I clear?"

Gretchen starts crying into her hands, but Jon ignores her and hauls me into the boss's office. "Sit."

He throws me into a chair and then tosses a blanket at me. I'm barely dressed, still wearing my stripping outfit. "What the hell is wrong with you?"

"With me?" I yell and jump up from my seat. "With me? You're seriously asking what's wrong with me—"

"Yes, I'm asking. You've been acting like a goddamn lunatic since the moment I saw you!" He's in my face, yelling down at me. My shoes are in the dressing room and my feet ache, my head aches, and my heart aches. I turn to leave. I'm not doing this right now. I can't. But Jon grabs my arm and stops me from walking away. "Where do you think you're going? You can't run away every time something doesn't go your way. You're not a child anymore, Cass."

"And neither are you!" I shove my palms into his chest, and then do it again, harder. "You can't fuck every girl who works here. That makes it a whorehouse and I'm not a fucking whore!" I try to hit him again, but he grabs my wrists.

"No one said you were." His voice softens. I try to pull away, but he won't let me. His lips are dangerously close and I'm aware of his scent, of the way his breathing is becoming more ragged, even though we've stopped yelling. His dark lashes are lowered, his blue eyes singularly focused on my mouth. "What happened to you, Cass?"

My lips part, but no words come out. How can I say it? How can I tell him? I shake my head and refuse to look up. Jon remains close enough that I can feel his warm breath. I want to lean into him, wrap my arms around his neck, and just cry until there are no tears left.

A hot wet tear slips from the corner of my eye and rolls down my cheek. Jon's thumb catches it and smoothes it away. "Talk to me Cass."

I make the mistake of looking up into his face. His heated gaze catches mine and I'm lost. His hand is still on my cheek and it happens so suddenly that I don't have time to think. Jon lowers his lips to mine and kisses me softly. The taste of his mouth, the way he holds me, makes me want more. The blanket falls to the floor and I step into his arms.

All the regrets I've ever had come boiling to the surface. I never gave him a chance. I wrote Jon off when we were younger and I shouldn't have. Our mouths press harder together, and his tongue slips into my mouth. I can barely breathe and I don't care. I don't stop to catch my breath. I kiss him harder, feeling his lips mash into mine as his hands travel down my back, tracing my bare skin. It's hotter than any kiss I've ever had. Jon presses his lips to mine like he'll never get the chance to do it again. There are no words that describe the longing I've felt for him, and what it means to feel him like this now—his body pressed firmly to mine, our lips tangling together as our tongues intertwine.

I have no plan of stopping, but a knock at the door forces us apart. My heart races hard as I jump away from him and grab the blanket off the floor. I walk to the corner of the room and pretend to look at something outside when the door opens. It's Bruce.

He pauses, and then says, "I need to know if these two are fired, boss. If you let them go, we have scheduling issues." Bruce lingers, waiting for an answer. I glance at Jon over my shoulder, not able to meet his eyes.

Jon is sitting on top of his desk, legs dangling off the side, leaning over with his head in his hands. He doesn't look up.

"Keep both of them, but no more warnings. If it happens again, with any of the girls, they're fired. Start to make a backup list of on-call dancers. Work them into the schedule so we have extra staff when we're shorthanded or someone calls in sick."

Bruce nods and leaves without another word. I find myself staring at Jon, wondering who he really is. I so much want the boy I knew to still be inside of him, but he was going to fuck Gretchen. Tucking my chin, I hurry past him. Maybe he is the boy I knew and maybe that's why I should stay away from him. Jon has no idea how badly he hurt me, or why I told the reporters who he was that summer in Mississippi. He doesn't know, and I'll never tell him.

As I reach for the door, he says, "I'm sorry."

I glance back at him. "For what?"

"I shouldn't have taken that from you. It wasn't—" He looks up at me from under thick lashes. "I know how you felt about things and I shouldn't have taken that kiss. I'm sorry, Cassie. It won't happen again."

I want to tell him, but I can't. He still hates me for what I did. I force a smile and look away. "Much more was taken from me than that. Besides, I gave it to you." I duck out the door before I can say more.

CHAPTER 29

JONATHAN

I avoid the club for the next few days because I can't stand the thought of seeing her there. My plan got fucked up the moment I made it. I didn't think about guys hanging on Cassie and saying they wanted to bend her over and have a good time. I didn't think about how I'd have to stand there and smile, like a fucking jackass, while they said these things about all the women working there. So, I've been going in during the day when Cassie doesn't work and going over things with Bruce. It's funny how fast the guy has my back. I doubled his salary, so maybe his reaction was predictable, but thank God for small wonders. I need something predictable right now.

"Why'd you buy a strip club?" Trystan is hanging upside down off the side of a club chair. His hair stands on end, sweeping against the dark carpet as he eyes the empty stage. It's early, and as soon as he heard what I did, Trystan came over to smack me in the head. "It looks better upside down, man."

I throw a phone book at him. It lands on his lap with a thud. Trystan shoots me a look and rights himself in the chair. "Seriously, Jon—this place is a fucking hole, your mother is going to kill you, and I can't hang out here. It'll totally ruin my reputation."

"What reputation?"

"That women come to me. Guys that dick around in strip clubs don't have women hanging off of them. Come on, Jon, what's this about? Did that asswipe get to you the other night? You didn't have to buy the club to get his ass fired. You know that right?"

I'm sitting at a nasty old desk, looking through an endless mountain of paper. The previous owner didn't believe in filing cabinets. I've been ignoring Trystan, not looking up, until he makes me by smacking the papers out of my hands. "What the hell is wrong with you? I need to go through this stuff and I don't have much time."

Trystan slams his hands on my desk and leans in. "Why?" A necklace slips out from the neck of his shirt. It's a silver band—a ring—dangling, spinning on its chain.

"Because I have other things to do and I can't be here—"

"Why?"

"Because!"

Trystan straightens and tucks the ring away so it can't be seen. He slips his hands into his pockets and turns, pacing the floor. A huge smile spreads across his face like he understands. "Oh, because. Yeah, that's a great explanation for acting like a crazy bastard." While he speaks, Trystan's index finger taps his chin, and his eyes flash like he knows damn well why I bought this place. The smirk falls off his mouth. Leaning against the wall, he folds his arms over his chest, and doesn't look at me. Long strands of dark hair block his face when he asks, "So, who is she?"

I stare at him. There's no point in denying it, he already knows something's up. I'm acting like a goddamn idiot, but I can't admit it. "No one, all right?"

"No one wouldn't make you act like this. You've been—shall we say, tense—since Peter's party, and I think I know why. That girl, the one he handed to you, the one you ran off with—she's the one that messed you up, isn't she?"

"Fuck, no. She's the one who patched me up." The words tumble out of my mouth before I can stop them.

Trystan is silent for a little bit. When he speaks he points out something I'd never thought about before. "You know why we're friends, right? Why we get along so well?" I glance at him, but Trystan's gaze doesn't meet mine. Instead he pushes off the wall and runs his hands through his hair. "There's no hiding what I lived through. The papers plastered it everywhere. Since then, I've found a few people who lived through their own hell, and it was always inflicted by someone else. You might not have said it, but there's something about people like us, Jon. We gravitate toward one another and try to protect each other."

I don't look at him. I know Trystan's been through the shitter and what his dad did to him. I don't disagree with him, although I have no idea what the hell he sees in me. I sound like a girl. I blink hard and look up at him. "You're like a brother to me, Trystan. You don't have to—"

"No, I think I do. You don't seem to realize what this girl means to you. She's seriously the one who put you back together?"

I nod and watch him as he sits on the edge of my desk. "Yeah, she was totally wrong for me." I smile, thinking about Cassie sitting at her Aunt's house and the way she smiled and danced around the place late at night when we were both too tired to sleep. "And yet..." I shrug, because there are no words—because she was and is the right woman for me. She always has been, which makes it hurt even more.

"You love her?"

The words hang there like a noose, waiting for me. It's always been waiting for me, and buying this place was like building the scaffolds so I can go hang myself. Rubbing my hands over my face, I say,

"Trystan, she stabbed me in the back. It doesn't matter how I feel about her because I can never trust again, not after that."

"Then, why'd you buy this place?"

"To save her from a little agony. Her life was hard before. I can't imagine what it's turned into for her to step out onto that stage every night. Maybe she meant to hurt me, but I can't leave her here like this. I want to make sure she's safe, and see what kind of asshole she married that will let her walk in here every night."

Grabbing a stack of papers, I slam them down on the desk and stand abruptly. I walk over to the window and look out into the dusty parking lot. This place is a dump and the thought of her being here is too much, but she's not mine to save. Cassie married someone else.

"Damn." Trystan pulls up one leg onto the desk and watches me for a second. I glance over my shoulder at him. "You're in love with the girl who got away—after she stabbed you in the back—who's married and works at a strip club. You're totally fucked. No wonder you've been acting like a madman." Trystan laughs, but it's not cruel. It's the laugher of the screwed.

"Yeah, no wonder."

CHAPTER 30

CASSIE

His kiss lingers long after it's gone. I'd always wondered what it would feel like to have Jon kiss me. God, I was so stupid when I met him. It's a wonder we got along at all. I think back and smile. Then I glance around at the basement apartment and dark paneling and I feel sick.

Grabbing a sweater, I shout to Beth, "I'm going for a walk."

"You're gonna get shot!"

"I'm fine. I'll be back in time for work. Don't leave without me." I'm out the door before she can reply or offer to come with me. I walk around to the side gate and when I look up I see the guy who gave me his inhaler.

Kam nods at me once, his dark eyes following me as I walk down the street. The park isn't too far from here. I suck in the cool air and let it fill my lungs until it feels like they're going to burst. Pulling my sweater tighter around me, I make my way into the little park and over to the swings. There's no one here right now. It's a bit too cool and damp to bring the toddlers out, and the older kids are still in school.

After wiping off the damp swing with my sleeve, I sit down. My head hangs between my shoulders as I study the way my shoes make lines in the clumpy sand. I wish I was able to fix my life, but wishing has never fixed anything. I can't divorce Mark without money, and it takes a lot more than I have. When I told my mom what happened, she didn't help me. She told me that I made this mess and I need to clean it up. As if I signed up to have a guy beat the shit out of me. Toby, my perfect older brother, agreed with her, and Dad's dead. There was no one to defend me, no one to offer me solace, or a place to rest my head when Mark tried to take it off my shoulders.

Things weren't bad at first. In the beginning, Mark was perfect. He didn't push me to do anything I didn't want to do. We'd stay up late and talk for hours, confessing our secrets. He made me happy. Mark didn't tell me that I was strange for wanting to wait to be with him until we were married. He held my hand and seemed content. Then came the wedding ring and when the honeymoon arrived, I was alone with him and Mark was a different man. The kind, patient person I fell in love with disappeared and I was left with someone else.

The first time we were together, I was so nervous that I couldn't do what he wanted. It was too much, too fast. I tried, but it hurt. I thought he'd let me stop, or slow down a little, but he didn't. His hand hit my face so hard that it left a mark. The next day when he was smiling at me over breakfast, I was too ashamed to tell anyone. I thought it was my fault.

Months passed and I was trapped. One time I tried to run away, but he found me. Mark showed up at work and got me fired. When I found out how much money I needed for a divorce, I didn't know what to do. Mark handled all the money. He didn't let me touch it, so I had nothing. He used my credit to buy things, he used my money, he used my body—he used me. It took me forever to figure out that he didn't love me.

I've never been so wrong about someone in my entire life, except maybe Jon. I never gave him a chance back then, and I regret it now. Seeing him again, tasting his lips like that, makes me realize how much I messed up. If I could take back what I did to him, I would.

A twig snaps, forcing my gaze to lift. I glance around for the source of the noise but there isn't anyone around. The park is empty, like it was before, but I can't shake the feeling that I'm being watched. The hairs on the back of my neck prickle, so I smooth it with my hand and glance around. Leaves rustle in the breeze, before a gray bunny hops out from behind a trash can.

I smile to myself for being paranoid. I always think every out of place sound is Mark sneaking up on me, even though I haven't seen him in a while. I'd like to feel safe again, someday. Pushing off the swing, I head back.

Beth is already dressed in a soft track suit with her bag over her shoulder. She's standing at the kitchen counter, stuffing a sandwich into her mouth as fast as possible. "Hurry up," she sputters, spewing crumbs everywhere.

"Why? It's still early."

"New boss wants us there now. We're late."

"The new boss. Right."

———

On the ride to work, I'm too quiet and Beth notices. She glances over at me. "So, are you ever going to tell me what went down between you two?"

"There's not much to tell."

"Liar. Just spill it. You'll feel better and facing him won't suck so much."

"Confession has never worked like that for me. It's always turned around and bitten me on the ass."

"Well, then you're doing it wrong." Beth blares the horn at someone and then bobs and weaves through traffic like she's possessed.

Gripping the door handle, I push myself back into the seat. "You might want to slow down a little."

"We're late."

"Fine, I'll tell you. Just slow down."

Beth gives me a wicked grin and then we both laugh as she resumes a normal driving speed. "So spill. Did you do it with him? Scorned lovers, right?"

Smiling, I shake my head and look at my fingernails. "No, it wasn't like that. We were friends, really good friends. The scar on my neck," I point to it, dragging my finger along the mark, "I got it when I was with Jon. There was a bombing and he saved me. His back is as cut up as my neck. If he didn't throw himself on top of me, I would have died. Someone else did. We were in the wrong place at the wrong time." I don't look up at her. My lashes remain lowered, my gaze locked on my fingers.

"So, then what's up with you two?"

I shrug. "I don't know."

"Cass…"

I don't want to tell her. It sounds horrible, and saying it out loud makes it worse. But I find the words and tell my story. "Fine, I do know. He hates me. I sold him out. At the end of the summer we spent together, a reporter wanted to know some things about the Ferros and had noticed me hanging around Jon all summer. I talked to him. He ran a story, and Jon never spoke to me again." Pressing my lips into a thin line, I try not to think about it. I was so naïve.

"What'd you tell the reporter?"

"Does it matter? It was enough to ruin whatever relationship we had." I sigh and lean my head against the window, watching the cars zip by.

"I'm sorry, but I can't believe you acted maliciously. You're too fucking nice to everyone. Did the guy trick you or something?" I wish he did, but it's not the truth. I shake my head and don't offer anything else. "Come on Cassie, there's gotta be—"

"There is no reason. Jon trusted me and I stabbed him in the back, okay? End of story. So now you know. Leave it alone." My throat tightens as the memories come flooding back. I can see the reporter, almost hear his voice. Confidence was strewn across my face as I answered him, certain that I was doing the right thing. Then I see the look on Jon's face when he found out, the blank stare that screams he can't believe I'd ever do something like that to him. But, I did. His uncle tossed my ass off their property before I could say anything. They never found out what happened, or why I did it.

When Beth pulls her car into the club parking lot, my heart races. Every inch of my body is tense, like I'm facing a firing squad, and I can't hide it. Beth pulls the keys from the ignition and turns to me. "And what else? Because there's something else. I'm not blind, Cass. Tell me."

I glance at her, quickly wishing that I could hide until this blows over, but it never seems to stop. There's always something else picking me clean, stripping me to the bone. I'm a mess of raw nerves and although she means well, I don't want to talk about it because there's nothing to say. It doesn't mean anything, not to Jon. Just before I push the door open, I tell her, "He kissed me last night."

CHAPTER 31

JONATHAN

Sean walks into the club just as I walk out. He slams into me, his palms shoving into my shoulders. "What have you done?" He glares at me with his condescending glare, as I stumble back from him.

"I'm not fighting with you." I shoulder past him, heading toward my car.

"Jonny," Sean says, grabbing my shoulder. "You'll talk now. Mom doesn't know yet, but she will by the time your ass hits her doorstep. Talk to me. What the hell are you doing? She's going to skin you, and run your carcass up the flagpole for this."

I glare at him. Sean and all his power, the way he's always two steps ahead, and every bit smarter than everyone else. I looked up to him once, but not anymore. "Thanks, I had no idea." My voice is flat and the words come out deadpan. I resist the urge to roll my eyes and turn to walk away, but Sean grabs my arm. "Don't fuck with me now, Sean."

My brother leans into my face and hisses, "Someone has to."

The way he says it makes my stomach sink. It's like he knows what I've done with Dad's mistresses, there's something in his voice—his eyes—that says so. "What do you want, Sean?"

He slips his hands into the pockets of his dark jeans and laughs, like something is funny. "I want what you want, little brother."

"Somehow I doubt that." An annoyed look crosses his features, but it's gone in a flash.

Leave it to Sean, he's the master of deception. I suppose he has to be that way or he'd hurl himself off a roof top. Still, when it's me and him, he can drop the act, but he never does. He's always Sean the omnipotent, the all-powerful Ferro brother. Screw that shit. The way I see it, he left me here to rot. If Peter hadn't come home, I wouldn't have seen Sean again. Never mind the fact that Sean had been in the city for weeks and didn't bother to visit me. I hadn't heard a word from him since he left here after Amanda died. I left Sean to wallow in his grief, and now he can leave me to stew in mine.

It's dusk and she'll be here soon, which is why I don't have time for Sean and his PMS. He follows behind me, talking, jabbing words at my back like harpoons. "You think you have to defy everyone. Does it make you feel like a man to piss all over the family name? Does it make you feel like you're worth something? Like you have power that the rest of us don't? Because, I wouldn't make that mistake, Jonny. Heir or not, you can be slammed back down into your quiet little place with one of Dad's bitches attached to your dick before sunset."

Sean's an asshole, but he usually means well. This time he doesn't. This time he's not testing, guiding, or doing any of that big brother shit he's pulled on me over the years. This time he sounds jealous and spiteful. My muscles tense and I keep walking, ignoring him until those last few words fall out of his mouth. They hit the ground like bombs and I explode. The satchel I have clutched under my arm is flung to the ground, and papers fly out as I ram into him, shoulder first.

Sean catches my arm and tries to pin it to my back, but I break free. Before he can speak, my fist collides with his mouth. The bastard is still talking, but I can't hear anything except the roaring of my pulse in my ears. We pound each other, twisting around on the ground, covered in dirt, until Trystan and Bryan pull us apart.

"What the fuck?" Bryan hisses at Sean, before smacking him in the back of the head. "Have you guys totally lost it?"

Sean swats at Bryan, but doesn't hit him. Instead, he glares at me as he bats the dust off his clothes. "Get rid of this. Now."

"So you can save face? Yeah, sure. Why not?" My voice is dripping with sarcasm that clearly conveys a different message—suck it.

Trystan is standing next to me. He tilts his chin up and asks Sean, "What's he looking at for something like this?"

"Disowned, if he's lucky." Sean looks over Trystan once, like he's no longer certain about the guy. When his gaze lands on me, he adds, "Peter will come by later with papers. Wait here for him, and sign the damn thing. Don't show your face until you do." Sean crosses the parking lot and glares at two girls who are headed toward the front door.

When I see who they are, my heart drops to my shoes. Trystan leans in and shoulders me, "Decide."

"What?" Blinking rapidly, I rub my temple and wipe away a bit of blood from where Sean's ring ripped open my skin. I avoid Cassie's gaze as she passes quickly. It's almost like she's running away from me.

"You see what's happening here, right?" Trystan hunches his shoulders forward and leans in. Bryan does the same thing, and places his hand on his chin, listening. "They're drawing lines, but they have no fucking clue why you're standing on this side."

"And they don't care, Jonny," Bryan adds quickly. "You're going to lose everything if you don't fix this. I mean, if Sean is trying to step in—"

Wiping my mouth with the back of my hand, I shake my head. "He's not trying to fix anything. Sean's after whatever Sean wants. He doesn't give a shit about me."

Trystan laughs and wraps his arm over my shoulder. "You're so amazingly wrong. I know what it looks like when people don't give a shit about you, and that wasn't it. Sean is trying to change your mind, although he's doing it wrong."

Bryan laughs like this whole mess is hysterical. Trystan and I stop walking and I look at him like he's gone nuts. Bryan holds his hand to his stomach, nearly doubled over. When he can breathe, he says, "I'm sorry, I just can't believe that I'm going to be the Ferro heir because you pissed off your mother and bought a strip club. Dude, you named it Club Ferro? You have a death wish. You have to. No one would be that mental, not around our family. Even this asshole knows that." He jabs his thumb at Trystan.

I glance at my car, and back at my newly acquired strip shack. I don't want to go back in there. I wonder if Cassie feels like that every time she steps into the place. Glancing at the guys out of the corner of my eye, I say, "Come on. Drinks are on me until Peter shows his face."

CHAPTER 32

CASSIE

I didn't expect to see Jon tonight, but he was standing in the parking lot when Beth and I passed. His eyes swept over me, like he couldn't stomach the sight of me. Nausea hits in a hard wave threatening to make me relive my cheap-o dinner.

Beth notices, but she doesn't say much as we dress. There are too many people around. The other girls who work the first shift are dressing quickly, and applying thick make-up.

Gretchen glares at me as she sprays her hair into place. I ignore her, and continue to get ready. I'm applying eyeliner when she leaves. As she walks by her hip bumps my elbow and I nearly stab my eye out. Stopping, she glances down at me. "Oops. Sorry, I didn't expect those beefy man arms to stick out quite so far." She walks past, swaying her hips with a smile on her lips.

"What a bitch," Beth says, and hands me make up remover to take off the jagged black line.

My eye won't stop watering, so I press my finger to the lower lid, trying to stop the flow of tears.

Bruce steps into the room and bellows at Beth, "Get on stage! And you," he points his sausage-sized finger at me, "Boss wants you in the pink room. Now. Move it."

Beth smiles at me before slipping away to reassure me that everything is going to be fine, but it's not. This is the end. I'm walking into his office and he's going to hand me my ass. I don't see why he hasn't done it already. After I finish dressing, I make my way to the pink room. When I get there, it's quiet. There's no one seated in front of the stage, no music blasting from the speakers. I'm wearing a corset that has my boobs ready to pop out over the top, along with matching bottoms, thigh highs, and stilettos.

My heart races faster as I step out onto the floor. "Hello?"

Someone moves in the back corner of the room and suddenly, I can see him. A man is standing, leaning against a dark wall, submerged in shadows. He steps toward me and my heart pounds harder. Jon.

"Hey, Cassie." He looks beaten, like life has sucked him dry and he can barely stand up.

"Are you okay?" I step toward him, wanting to touch the gash on his face, but I think twice and keep my distance.

Jon's blazing blue eyes sweep over me, drinking me in like he'll never see me again. He doesn't answer my question. Looking at the floor, he says, "The pink room is closed tonight."

I manage to keep a plastic smile plastered on my face, right up until he says that. "Oh. Am I... supposed to work a different room?" My stomach is twisting into knots.

Jon shakes his head, and then lifts his chin and pushes his dark hair away from his eyes. "No, not tonight."

"Jon, are you firing me?" My heart thumps inside my chest like this can't be happening.

His eyes sweep over my face, but I can't read his expression. He seems so somber, like someone died. "Why are you working here?" I stiffen, my defenses rising, but Jon steps toward me and rests his hands on my bare shoulders. He's strong and careful. He smiles sadly at me, and says, "I need to know what happened to you."

"Nothing worth repeating." I smile weakly, and then drop his gaze knowing that my answer is too weak. We have no relationship, not anymore, but I wish—just for one second—that I could start over. Such hopes are useless, which is why I usually bat them away as soon as they flood my mind, but not tonight. Tonight I want to fix the unfixable. I want another chance with him, but there's no way. Jon would be an idiot to give it to me. There's no way he'll ever trust me again. Not after the things I did to him.

Sucking in a deep breath, I step forward saying, "You were right. My ideals, the way I wanted to live my life, were lacking a dose of reality. I was so naïve—"

"No, you weren't. I just said that so I'd get a shot with you." He smiles at me, but it's hollow. It's a mingling of regret masked by humor and I hear it choking him when he says the words.

Jon presses his eyes closed for a second and when he looks at me again it feels like someone's sucked all the air out of the room. The way he looks at me sends a jolt of hope straight into my heart. It's almost too much to witness, but I don't look away—I can't.

Swallowing hard, his voice is barely a whisper when he speaks, "I was in love with you, Cassie. I never had a chance, so of course I'd say whatever I could to get you to look at me that way." The soft lines on his face harden as his expression turns rancid. "But you never did, did you? I was always something expendable." The pencil in his hand cracks, but neither of us acknowledges the sound.

The insides of my ears throb. I heard the words, but I can't believe them. I stare at him, leaning forward like he's using an invisible lure to reel me in. I can't fight with him anymore, and things can't end this way, and this clearly feels like the end for us. My pulse pounds faster as I blink away tears and slap a smile across my face to hide my pain. "You weren't expendable. I would have kept you around forever. I would have—"

Shaking his head, Jon steps toward me. "But you didn't. You told the press where I was, what I'd done. You knew what that meant, what would happen to me, and you did it anyway. Why? Just tell me why so I can walk away from you and know the truth." As he speaks, he takes my hands and presses them to his face. It's like he's begging me to release him, but I never knew he was mine.

My lips part, jaw dropping open as my heart is ripped out of my chest. Is it true? Was he really in love with me? I remain on my feet even though my knees are ready to go out. My throat tightens so much that it's difficult to speak. "I tried to tell you, but your uncle wouldn't let me see you. Then you were gone before I could explain. Jon, I meant to help you. I thought I was helping you. Everything the press wrote about you at the time was wrong—like horribly wrong. They had no idea how smart and compassionate you were. They only printed crap about your latest conquest or screw up. I thought if I told them the truth—I thought if I told them who you really are—that they'd see it, too."

He stares at me, wide-eyed, shocked. His hands drop to my arms. "You didn't tell them that I bought a high school to sleep with that girl? Or those things about my dad's mistress?" He wants to believe me, but I can see that he's not going to. It doesn't matter what I say. Too much time has passed, and anguish has consumed any chance we had.

I try anyway, because the truth can't make it worse. Not now. "A guy gave me a card right before we left the hospital. He knew that we went to the exhibit together and thought we were, uh, intimate. I didn't talk to him then. I knew what you said, how you needed to avoid the press, so I didn't talk to him. But I didn't like it. The papers kept running stuff on you, even when you were with me, making up stories about how you were fucking your way through Europe.

"So, I called the reporter, and I told him about you and the school, and the way you spoke of their curriculum—and the way you knew about Jonathan Gray's art work. I told them how you protected me at his show—and how you helped the others who were hurt. That old lady survived because of you. At the end of the day you were covered in blood and you didn't even care about your own safety. You never do, Jon. You always put other people first."

I smile sadly at him. "I told the reporter how you helped Aunt Paula, and how you helped me. I told him the Jonathan Ferro they printed stories about didn't exist, that there was this other side to him, a side that's good, a side that he keeps hidden. That was what I said. I told them to run that story."

His fingers tighten on my forearms before he releases me and looks away. Pushing his hair out of his eyes, he asks, "And he didn't, did he?"

I shake my head. "No, he didn't." Out of all the stupid things I've done, that was the dumbest. I never saw it coming until my words showed up in the paper, their meaning twisted, and showcasing Jon as the playboy troublemaker that the world loves and wants. Scandals sell papers, not altruistic young men.

Jon presses his fingers to the bridge of his nose and turns away from me suddenly. "It doesn't make sense. You talked to the reporter—you called him—and he ran other information, things you didn't tell him?"

"I don't remember telling him some of the things he wrote, but I must have. I did mention there was a girl you liked, which is how you knew about her school. He must have read into it. Jon, I'm sorry. If I could take it all back, I would. I never meant to hurt you."

Jon's back is turned to me, his lungs filling with air as anger takes hold. These were words I could never say—he didn't give me the chance. And now, I almost regret saying them because everything that happened afterward was my fault.

Jon rounds on me, his eyes blazing, and steps so close that his breath feels like wind on my face. "Well, you did."

His eyes lock with mine as my pulse roars in my ears and tears gather in the corners of my eyes. I destroyed him. My stupidity ruined his life. A single thoughtless act brought about a chain reaction of events, and the wrath of his mother, in a way that was unforeseeable to me. But it doesn't matter, because when life gets bad like that, we all need someone to blame and Jon blames me, good intentions or not. The fury on his face speaks for him, but I can't step away. I'm trapped. Even though I'm standing inches from his arms, I'm miles from his heart. I'll never be close to him again and it's my own damn fault.

The clock ticks loudly on the wall. The seconds pass, dragging on for what feels like hours, as we stand like that. His breath washes over my face as he works his jaw, his lips pressing into a thin line over and over again, as if he's biting back words that want to slaughter me. But he says nothing. Every inch of my skin is charged. I want to take him in my arms so much, but I can't. After everything that happened, here we are, years later, but it feels like that day all over again. Except that time I didn't get the chance to explain. I imagined this moment so many times, and never did it end like this.

The hollow spot in the center of my chest feels like it's being blasted with bricks. I can't breathe and I have no idea how I'm still standing here, facing him. There's one thing I never told him, one thing I couldn't manage to confess, and since it's clear that I'm never going to see him again, I say it.

The words come out like an apology, soft and confession-like. "You had a better grasp on life back then, and I was too stupid to see that the thing that I wanted most in the world was you. I loved you then and I've never stopped." My voice trails off as I say the last sentence. Hot tears roll down my cheeks as I avert my eyes and confess my feelings to his shoulder, and then to the floor.

My voice catches in the back of my throat as I draw back a foot, ready to turn away. "That's why I called them—I adored you and I wanted the world to see the man that I saw. I'm sorry, Jon. It's too little, too late, but it's all I have to offer."

As I turn to step away, his arm juts out and his fingers wrap around my wrist. When he speaks, I stare at his hand because I can't look into his hope-drained eyes.

"You married someone else, even though you loved me?"

"Yeah," I laugh bitterly. "I thought I'd move on and get over you, but things don't work like that, do they?" I chance it and look up at him from under wet lashes.

His deep blue gaze ensnares me and our eyes lock. Jon shakes his head, and when I look away, he takes my chin in his hand, gently turning my face back to him. Soft touches while fighting are so foreign that I flinch when he reaches for me. Lines crease his face like he knows why I'd flinch, like he knows what it implies. "What happened to you Cassie? What'd he do to you?"

My lower lip quivers because I don't want to remember, but everything comes flooding back. The reality of Jon's kind words and gentle touches crash into Mark's distorted affection. My lip quivers as I try to tell him, but no words come out. Tears streak down my cheeks, unbidden and unwanted, as I look away. "I should go," I manage to say.

His eyes lower to the floor and he nods. Jon doesn't say anything as he follows me to the door. When I reach for the handle he steps closer, his back nearly touching mine as his hand lands above my shoulder, preventing me from leaving.

He speaks to my back, quickly, like he knows he's out of time. "I don't want things to end this way, but I have no idea how to fix them. You're married, Cass. I'm in love with a married woman who ruined years of my life. Maybe I have no sense, but I can't let you go."

My back tenses because I've been in this position before. In the past my hands have flown up to protect my face, as fists were punched into the wall next to my head. There are no such things as do-overs. Reality doesn't grant second chances, but for some reason, Jon is. My heart thuds harder inside my chest as I stand there trying not to shake, but it doesn't work.

Jon takes my shoulder and turns me toward him, his touch is kind and careful, like I'm made of glass. He presses his forehead to mine and wipes the tears off my cheeks. "Don't leave me, Cass."

The touch is so tender, so perfect, that I'm paralyzed. It's what I crave, what I need so desperately. Jon's fingers tangle in my hair as his thumbs wipe away tears, and he tilts my face up. His eyes lock on my lips, which makes my body run warm. The magnetic pull is strong, but neither of us moves. We're locked in place, fighting the attraction. When Jon breaks my gaze, he pulls me into his chest, embracing me, whispering in my ear, "I can't even kiss you. This is torture, Cass. I want you so much, but you belong to someone else."

My mind is blubbering, running nonsensical thoughts through my head, trying to grasp what's happening here. I speak into his shoulder, holding onto him tight, confessing the things nightmares are made of, "He thinks I'm his, too. He says that I should do what he tells me and not complain, that I have it good with him."

"So, did you?" Jon pulls back enough to see my face. One of his hands gently sweeps over my cheek, pushing away stray hairs that were stuck to my damp skin. "I mean, do you love him? Because if you're happy Cass—then I don't want to—"

"I'm hiding from him. That's why I work here, because it's the only job I could find that pays enough and has a security guard to protect me. But he's looking for me, Jon. He'll drag me back there and I don't want to go back. I can't go back." I'm no longer blinking. Instead, I'm staring off into space, reliving the hell I escaped from as my body shivers because I'm unable to repress the memories.

"He hurt you." There's no question in Jon's voice. He knows, he's sure of his statement.

I nod, almost too ashamed to say it, and look at the floor. "It was my fault—"

"Cassie, baby, look at me." Jon takes my face in his palms and raises my gaze until I have to look at him. "No matter what happened, no matter what you did, he shouldn't have hurt you." Sobs are bubbling up from inside of me, but I choke them back down.

His hands run through my hair, stroking gently as a smile spreads across his face. "You completely messed up my life. If anyone had the right to punish you for what you've done, it's me. So maybe I'm a fucked up asshole, but I want to hold you in my arms and kiss you breathless. I want you by me every moment of every day. And these tears," his eyes drift to my cheek, "I want to kiss them away and make sure they never come back."

Jon's gaze follows a tear as it slips down my cheek. Leaning in slowly, he brushes his lips to the tear, kissing it away. I close my eyes, as I tense and hold my breath. Those warm lips feel so soft and perfect against my skin. Jon does it again, leaning in close to the other side of my face, and kissing away another tear. He does it over and over, each time slower than the last, letting his lips linger longer, until he works his way to the spot where the tears collect at the corner of my lips.

When Jon leans in for that kiss, my heart lurches and slams into my ribs as my body is covered in a rush of heat. The sensation of his mouth so close to mine makes me turn my head the slightest bit so that we're lip to lip.

Jon watches me from beneath lowered lashes, his gaze locked on my mouth. "Can I kiss you, Cassie?"

CHAPTER 33

JONATHAN

She's trembling, standing half naked in front of me. Vulnerability is painted across her beautiful face and I'm a dick for doing this to her now, but I can't stop. The pull is too strong and before I know what's happening, I'm standing before her, wanting to cover her body in light kisses. I nearly do it, but then I stop. I don't want to add to whatever hell she's been through, and from the way she flinched when I moved before, I know that fucker did something to her. Cassie isn't saying much about him, but I know what I see, and I see that she's been wounded. I want to take away her pain, just for a second, so I ask her for a kiss.

Her big brown eyes lock on mine, and Cassie nods once. The movement makes that silky dark hair fall over her bare shoulders. Her beautiful body shivers as she fights for breath in that corset. God, I want to rip it off of her. Gently, gently, I chant over and over again in my mind. She doesn't need another asshole using her, but as I think it, I know it's not true. I don't want to use her—I want her for myself. I love her.

As I lean in, I can't stop looking at her mouth, wondering what those big full lips will feel like if I kissed her as deeply as I want to. The woman is an emotional train wreck. Something inside my head is screaming at me to stop and be her friend. God knows she needs one, but those pink lips call to me and I can't pull away. I'm trapped and I don't want to leave this place. My mind is hers, my body is hers, every bit of me—I'd give it to her and worship at her feet if she'd let me in the way she used to.

My body buzzes with feverish intensity as my mouth touches hers. When her lashes close and her lips part, I can't resist. I mean, I try. I try to give her a long, slow, gentle kiss, but with her arms wrapped around my chest and her nails biting into my back, it's hard to go slow. Tracing my tongue over the swell of her lower lip, I kiss her softly, making her moan into my mouth. Cassie leans into me, and presses her tight little body against my chest even harder.

I'm lost in a spray of sparks as the intensity of the kiss escalates. Tingles run through me, making my desire for her impossible to hide. My lips dance with hers, tasting her, drinking her in like I'll never have this chance again. Her tongue flicks across the seam of my lips and I let her in as her fingers tangle in my hair, kissing me deeper, harder. Pressing my body against hers, I push her into the wall as my hands trail down the sides of the lingerie and over her bare hips. I moan into her mouth as she kisses me and her fingers tug at my hair, like I'm not close enough. Cassie nips my lip playfully and I take her head in my hands and kiss her with every last bit of passion I can offer. I don't hold back. I don't mask how much I want her or what she does to me. She can feel it—my ragged breathing, my hot body, and my dick straining for her touch—and she doesn't slink back.

We're tangled together like that, lost in a kiss that feels hotter than Hell when someone knocks on the door. My heart is ready to burst when we fly apart. Cassie's eyes are wide as she wipes away the kiss with the back of her hand, her expression panicked.

Ignoring the knock, I step toward her and whisper, "Are you okay?" I watch her closely, seeing the rapid pace of her breathing as her breasts swell over and over again as she gasps for air. She nods and seems lost for a moment. Her lips part like she wants to say something, but there's a knock at the door again, louder this time.

"Come on, Jonny. Open the door." Peter's voice comes through the thin wood, and I know he's leaning against the frame. If Sean showed up with him, they would have walked in on us. Unlike Sean, Peter has some manners. "I need to talk to you."

I grab my jacket from the back of the door and slip it over her shoulders. Cassie takes it, holding it in front of her, just under her chin. When I open the door, Peter is standing there with Bryan.

Bryan grins at me, like he knows what we were up to. Peter is too polite to comment. They walk inside and Cassie starts to leave. I reach for her, afraid that she'll go and I'll never see her again. "Stay."

"Are you sure?"

I nod and look at the guys. "Yeah, please, sit." Cassie glances at Peter, uncertain, and then makes her way to a seat. I toss her a blanket and she wraps it over her shoulders, but it doesn't cover all of her. Bryan's eyes scan her legs so I smack him in the head. "Stop looking."

Bryan's face turns red and he looks the other way. "I wasn't."

Peter cuts us off. "So, you bought a strip club and risked your inheritance."

Bryan snorts, "Risked? Peter, call it what it is. He's fucked. As soon as his mother finds out, he's toast." He leans back in his chair with a smile on his face, threading his fingers behind his head. "I've always wanted to be the heir. Thanks, cousin."

Peter slaps Bryan in the back of the head, which makes him drop the smug look and sit upright. "You won't be the heir because you knew about it. Mom will castrate you, too."

Bryan smiles like money doesn't matter, like nothing matters except sunlight, fresh air, and fun. "Yeah, probably."

Peter rolls his eyes and his tension becomes more visible. He slaps down a yellow envelope on the desk and presses a finger to it. While looking at me, he explains, "Sean—no matter how obnoxious and condescending he is—was watching your back. Mom's been tied up in meetings all week and doesn't know, yet. And, what Sean arranged makes this whole thing go away. There are papers in here that will expunge the previous transaction. All you have to do is sign them."

Bryan looks between us as Peter speaks. My arms fold over my chest, but I'm not sure why I don't like this. Maybe it's pride, but I don't think so. So I don't sign. Instead, I'm silent and glaring.

Bryan finally says something. "You should sign that, Jonny. And then kiss Sean's ass."

Ignoring him, I ask Peter, "Why do you think I bought this place?" Thrusting out my hand, I gesture for the papers and Peter hands them to me. I glance at them, while he speaks. The thing is, I know what he thinks. I know what they all think.

Peter sighs and tucks his hands into the crooks of his arms as he folds them across his chest. "Does it matter? This is so over the top, even for you, that you had to know what Mom would do to you when you bought the place."

The porcelain skin on Cassie's face wrinkles and she leans forward in her chair. "You were serious? Buying this place will get him disowned?"

Peter nods slowly, his eyes burning a hole into my head, demanding an answer that I won't give. "Yes. He's been on thin ice for a while, and finally was given an ultimatum that if he did one more thing to sully the Ferro name, he was done. He'll be stripped of his birthright and tossed out on his ass."

Why'd he have to tell her that? I laugh and toss the papers back at him. Peter catches them and looks shocked. "No. I'm not signing these. Tell Sean, thanks, but no thanks."

"You realize that you can't win, right?" Bryan is on his feet, his serious expression making him look years older. "You bought this place with Ferro money. They'll keep it when they toss you, Jon. If you sign the papers, you lose the building but keep your fortune."

"It's not about the building or the fortune." I say, and turn away from them. Their eyes are on my back, I feel them judging me even though they have no idea what compels me to do anything.

"Then what's it about?" Peter asks, stepping toward me. "Talk to me, Jon." I don't mean to, but my gaze flicks to Cassie as I glance up at Peter. He turns and looks at her, his expression softer than most. "Who are you?"

"Cassie Hale."

Peter blinks like the name means something, and it should. Cassie Hale was the woman who nailed me into my self-made coffin three years ago. The press slaughtered me and threw me inside. The repercussions still send tremors through the family even now—the things that were printed about my mother were enough to rip apart other families.

Peter's eyes go wide with recognition. He looks at me and blinks like he took a fist to the face. Pointing at her, he says, "Are you serious? You're slaughtering yourself for her?"

I'm not mad at him, because he doesn't understand. He saw how much pain she caused me back then, but he doesn't know what he's talking about. I open the door, a cue for him to leave, "Thanks Pete, but tell Sean that I can handle myself."

Peter nods. He won't start a fight, he's not like that. Instead he walks to the door and stops in front of me. "I'll help you, Jonny. Anything you need, I'm there. But you have to realize the shit storm that's going to fall on your shoulders. Everything will come out, and I mean everything." His gaze holds mine and I know what he means—the mistresses. Fuck, does everyone know about that?

"Thanks, Pete." I place my hand on his shoulder and go to say more, but lose my train of thought when I look through the door. I do a double take, because what I'm seeing can't possibly be real. Two brunettes are on stage, wearing really short daisy dukes. They have on men's dress shirts that are tied right under their breasts, with only one button closed so you can see the top of their bras, and quite a bit of cleavage. One has long pin-straight hair, while the other is curly and all over the place as she whips it around.

The club is closed for the night. Bruce sent the staff home, and most of the lights have been shut off, except for the main stage where Peter's fiancée is dancing with another woman. They're both laughing and swishing those long locks in circles. Sidney giggles and nearly falls off the stage, but the other woman steadies her and they both laugh so hard that they don't notice us gaping at them.

Bryan grins when he sees the display in the front of the stage. Trystan is leaning back in a chair, like he's hoping a portal will open up and suck him into the afterlife, while a girl with caramel skin squeezes his cheeks and hysterically paws at him, repeating the same phrase over and over again, "Holy shit! It's Trystan Scott!"

The dancer that I don't recognize says over her shoulder, "Yeah Mel, you said that already."

I stare, and finally find my voice, "Is that Sidney?"

A slow smile stretches across Peter's face and he laughs. "Yeah, and the one standing next to her is Avery Stanz, the woman that has your brother totally whipped."

STRIPPED #2
COMING SOON

To ensure you don't miss the release of STRIPPED #2 text **AWESOMEBOOKS** (one word) to **22828** and you will get an email reminder on release day.

Turn the page to read a FREE sample of the bestselling series: THE ARRANGEMENT

THE ARRANGEMENT

Vol. 1

By

H.M. Ward

CHAPTER 1

The night air is frigid. It doesn't help that I'm stuck wearing this little black dress in my crap car. I shiver as I try to keep the engine running at a red light. My little battered car is from two decades ago and stalls if I don't rev the engine while I have my foot on the brake. I'm driving with two feet, in a car that's supposed to be an automatic. The heater doesn't work. If I try to turn it on, I'll get my face blasted with white smoke. It's awesome, in an utterly humbling kind of way. At least the car is mine. It gets me where I need to go, most of the time.

The light flips to green and I botch it. I don't gas the car enough and it shutters and stalls. I grumble and grab for the can of ether. The cars behind me blare their horns.

I ignore them. They can go around me. I grab the can on the seat next to me, kick open my door, and walk around to the hood. I shake the can and spray it into the engine intake. The car will start up as soon as I turn the key now, and I can drive away in shame.

The night air is crisp and filled with exhaust. This road is always busy. It doesn't matter what time of day it is. Angry drivers move around me. Everyone is always in a hurry. It's part of the New York frame of mind. I'm treated to a catcall as a car full of guys blows past me. I flip them the bird and hear their laughter echo as they fade from sight.

Tonight couldn't possibly get any worse. I put the cap on the can of ether. Then it happens. My night takes a one-eighty straight into suckage.

As I drop the hood, it slams shut, and I look through the windshield. "Seriously?" I say at the guy who jumps in my seat. He's wearing a once-blue fluffy coat and hasn't shaved for weeks. He turns the key and my crappy car roars to life. He gasses it and takes off, swerving around me. I stand in the lane staring after him. What a moron. Who'd steal that piece of trash?

Still, it's my car and I need it. After the night I had, I don't want to run after him, but I have to. I need that car. I take off at a full run. My lungs start to burn as I suck in frozen air and exhaust. I run down the shoulder, avoiding trash that's laying in the gutter. My attention is singularly focused on my car. I push my body harder and feel my muscles protest, but I don't hold back. He's getting away.

I manage to run a block when a guy on a motorcycle slows next to me. "That guy stole your car." He sounds shocked.

I can't see his face through the black helmet. It has a tinted visor that covers his face. "No shit, Sherlock," I huff and keep running. My purse is in the car, my only pair of work acceptable heels, my books—awh, fuck—my books. I paid over a grand for those. They're worth more than the car. I run faster. My dress flares around my thighs as my Chucks help me sprint forward. My body doesn't want to do it. The stitch in my side feels like it's going to bust open.

The guy on the bike is annoying. He rolls next to me and flips up his face shield.

I glance at him, wondering what he's doing. Biker guy looks at me like I'm crazy. "Are you trying to catch him?"

"Yes," pointing ahead, huffing. There are three lights on this stretch of road before the ramp to get on the parkway. If he hits a red light, the car will stall and I'll get it back. My lungs are burning and it's not like I have time to explain this. My car has already passed the first light. "If he stops, the car will stall."

"You want me to help?" he glances at the car and then back at me.

I stop and nearly double over. Holy hell, I'm out of shape. I nod and throw my leg over the back of his bike, flashing the cars driving past us. I so don't care. Wrapping my arms around his waist, I hold on tight and say, "Go."

"I was going to call the cops, but this works, too." He sounds amused. I hold onto his trim waist and plaster myself against his back. He's wearing a leather jacket, and I can feel his toned body through the supple material. He pulls into traffic and zips through the lanes. The wind blasts my hair and plasters my eyelashes wide open. We bob and weave, getting closer and closer to my car. My heart is racing so fast that it's going to explode.

I see my car. It's passing the second light. Motorcycle man punches it, and the bike flies under the second intersection just as the light changes. I manage not to shriek. My skirt flies up to my hips, but I don't let go of the biker's waist to push the fabric back down.

We're nearly there when the thief catches the third light. The car in front of him stops, forcing the carjacker to stop as well. As soon as he takes his foot off the gas, my car convulses and white smoke shoots out the tailpipe. The engine ceases. The driver's side door is kicked open and the guy runs.

Motorcycle man pulls up next to my car. I slip off the back of the bike, my heart beating a mile a minute. I can't afford to lose this stuff. I'm barely making it as it is. I look at my car. Everything is still there. I turn back to the guy on the bike as I smooth my skirt back into place.

Tucking my hair behind my ear, I say, "Thanks." I must seem insane.

He flips his face shield up and says, "No problem. Does your car always do that?" A pair of blue eyes meets mine and the floor of my stomach gives way. Damn, he's cute. No, not cute—he's hot.

"Get jacked? No, not always."

He smiles. There's a dusting of stubble on his cheeks. I can barely see it because of the helmet. He raises an eyebrow at me and asks, "This has happened before, hasn't it?"

More times than you'd think. Criminals are really stupid. "Let's just say, this isn't the first time I had to chase after the car. So far no one's made it to the parkway. That damn light takes forever and I keep stalling out in the same spot. You'd think I'd figure it out by now, but…" But I'm mentally challenged and prefer to chase after car thieves. I stop talking and press my lips together. His eyes run over my dress and pause on my sneakers, before returning to my face. Great, he thinks I'm mental.

Turning to the car, I grab another can of ether from the backseat and walk around to the front. I dropped the last can somewhere behind me. I pop the hood and spray. I'm so cold that I've gone numb. As

I walk back to my door, I shake my head saying, "Who steals a car that barely runs?"

"Do you need any help?" The guy holds my gaze for a moment and my stomach twists. He seems sincere, which kills me. A strange compulsion to spill my guts tries to overtake me, but I bash it back down.

Pressing my lips together, I shake my head, and swallow the lump in my throat. Today sucked. I'm totally alone. No one helps me, and yet this guy did. "No, I'm okay," I lie as I slip into my car and yank the door shut. "Thanks for the ride." I turn the engine over and smile at him. The window is down. It doesn't go up.

"Anytime." He nods at me, like he wants to say something else. All I can see of his face is his crystal blue eyes and a beautiful mouth. He's sitting on a bike that cost more than my tuition. He's loaded and I've got nothing. A pang of remorse shots through me, but I need to go. The haves and the have-not weren't made to mingle. I already learned that lesson once. I don't need to learn it again.

"Thanks," I say before he can ask my name. "I'll see you around." I smile at him and drive away, holding back tears that are building behind my eyes.

It's weird. There are so many shitty people in the world, and on the worst day of my life, I finally find a nice one and I'm driving away from him.

THE ARRANGEMENT 1

is on sale now

MORE BOOKS BY H.M. WARD

THE ARRANGEMENT:
THE FERRO FAMILY

DAMAGED: THE FERRO FAMILY

DAMAGED 2: THE FERRO
FAMILY

SCANDALOUS

SECRETS

THE SECRET LIFE OF TRYSTAN
SCOTT
And more.

To see a full book list, please visit:

www.SexyAwesomeBooks.com/books.htm

CAN'T WAIT FOR H.M WARD'S NEXT STEAMY BOOK?

Let her know by leaving stars and telling her what you liked about STRIPPED in a review!